AF432152

Seraphim Bloodlines

KATHLEEN I. LYONS

Seraphim Bloodlines

Kathleen I. Lyons

For those who feel unseen, for those who struggle with the weight of their own mental distress, know that you are not alone. This book is dedicated to you. Have strength and courage as you move forward.

Stand strong together,

BEFORE YOU READ

This book has some themes and happenings that may be triggering for the reader. These include but are not limited to childhood trauma, survivor's guilt, psychological manipulation through gas-lighting as well as supernatural abilities, mentions of plans for sexual assault as well as implied sexual assault, panic attacks, etc.

If these topics make you feel uncomfortable and psychologically itchy (as I like to say), then please be cautious.

PROLOGUE

Eighteen Years Ago

Luka

I gently pet the young girl's head as she slept; the poor thing must have been walking a very long time to still be asleep after two days. I was thinking I should have taken her to a hospital instead of bringing her into my home.

"She's still not awake?"

I looked over my shoulder to see my partner, Avery. He had just come back down from making sure my younger brother was asleep. I could only imagine how curious Brine was, but I didn't want him to worry; he was still a kid.

But then again, so was this girl, and she was certainly a strong girl to have survived whatever she did.

I sighed and looked back at the girl, gently brushing my fingers through her white hair that was tarnished by ash and soot.

"She's still breathing, thank Gods," I said, "but I'm concerned. I'm no doctor, but I would have thought that she was in a coma."

"Well, it's a good thing you're not a doctor." Avery chuckled, trying to lighten the mood as he came over and gently put his hand on my shoulder, his thumb softly stroking my arm. "I'm honestly surprised you've not taken her to a hospital already, though."

"You know me, Avery." I said, a smile spreading across my lips as I put my hand on his. "I couldn't leave her alone like that. She was just... wandering the street..."

"She's not a puppy, love." He said, his other hand stroking my other arm affectionately. "With how things are, we can't take care of her... we need to call the cops."

"And tell them what, Avery?" I asked, looking at him. "You know that the first thing they'll ask is where we found her, and the next will be why we didn't immediately take her to the hospital."

"And why *didn't* you take to the hospital when you found her, Luka?" He asked. "Why risk bringing her back here?"

I didn't know how to explain it to him; it was a feeling in my gut that led me to do what I did. It told me *I* was supposed to be the one to take care of her. The girl needed the calm face of someone who was truly concerned, not the face of some doctor or nurse that just wanted to poke and prod her with needles and run tests.

She needed someone who cared, and even though the two of us were perfect strangers, I wanted to let her know that someone did care about her.

Before I could even answer, there was a knock at the door, and my body went rigid in defense, my teeth almost bared. Avery's hands tightened on my shoulders; his guard was up as well.

Had someone seen me bring the girl here and thought the worst?

No, no one in this neighborhood would call the cops.

This was the Outer Districts, practically a lawless part of Arboriah City, and the cops that "patrolled" the streets didn't care about anything that happened to the citizens that lived here.

Our defensive nature quickly transformed into confusion, however, when a soft voice like that of a bell spoke through the door.

A woman's voice.

"I mean neither of you any harm, Mr. Coltt and Mr. Malcolm." She spoke. "I am only here to make sure that the child you found is okay."

It wasn't a voice that I recognized, and I looked at Avery, wondering what he thought of the situation. He simply shrugged his shoulders, a sign that he was leaving the decision for me to decide. I took a deep breath and stood from where I'd been kneeling. I slowly made my way to the front door.

I paused as I put my hand on the doorknob, not knowing what I would find on the other side. But whether the person on the other side of the door was a concerned individual or someone who meant her harm, I knew I couldn't keep whoever was standing out there waiting.

"Your heart is in the right place, Mr. Coltt." The voice said, startling me from my thoughts. "I assure you, I mean none of you any harm. After I am certain that the girl is okay and will be safe here, then I will leave here."

I was curious, but my brow furrowed all the more; how had she known that I was the one standing at the door and not Avery?

I opened the door to find a woman on our doorstep, and she was wearing very odd clothing; she was wearing a light blue riding cloak, the kind that I'd seen in the Historical District of the city. She had the whitest hair I'd ever seen, and I'd almost thought she was a fellow vampire had it not been for her eyes.

Her eyes were not the color of rubies like that of a vampire or any generation or ancestry that I knew of; they were cyan blue; and they almost seemed like glass marbles.

She stood like that of a noble lady, and her posture was definitely the kind to demand respect. However, I didn't sense any hostility from her; she had a clean air about her.

"Who are you?" I asked without thinking.

She smiled softly at me and bowed her head.

"My name has been lost to time, I am afraid." She spoke with an accent, and her vernacular reminded me of stories performed in a theater. "I guess you could say... that I am someone who is concerned about that girl's well-being, but I cannot do what I can for her, considering my current predicament."

I pride myself in being an excellent judge of character, and from the look on this woman's face and how she carried herself, I knew she was telling the truth.

I stood with Avery as the mysterious woman knelt at the side of the sleeping girl on my couch. Seeing how she cared for her, I would have sworn that the two of them were related; the girl's hair was just as white as the woman's, and they shared the same pale skin.

'I wonder if the girl has the same glass-like eyes.'

"How do we know that this woman is really here to help?" Avery muttered to me, his tone defensive.

"I can't explain it." I muttered back. "But I do know that she's telling the truth."

The woman hummed softly as she gently combed her fingers through the girl's hair. The touch was almost... motherly.

"Who is she to you?" I asked, deciding to ask what had been on mine and Avery's minds since the woman had arrived.

The woman stood and turned to us, a soft smile on her pale lips.

"This child is very dear to me." She said, her smile faltering a little as she looked down. "As is her twin sister... but she was taken away, taken by someone who seeks to destroy this city and what the First Council fought so hard to protect."

She looked up at us, her gentle face having grown serious.

"My daughters have both been pulled into something that even I cannot fully understand... and this conflict will mold them both into enemies... I thought I could prevent it... but I was wrong..."

Avery and I shared a look of confusion as we looked at each other, the woman's words carrying a mysterious weight to them. The concern I had was now growing into dread in the pit of my stomach. I looked at her again.

"Who are you?" I again asked the beginning of many questions that I needed the answers to.

The woman's sad smile returned, and she crooned.

"My name is..."

I stared at the girl on my couch as the woman's words replayed in my mind, the gravity of the situation becoming more and more clear. The woman explained a great deal to Avery and me, and when her explanations were finished, she bowed and left the house, wishing us the best and trusting us with the care of the child.

'A conflict that threatens to destroy the very foundation of the city.'

'The return of a bygone horror.'

At first, I didn't want to believe any of it, but the more I thought about it, the more it made sense.

Well, to me, at least.

"Luka, are we really sure about this?" Avery asked. "Are we really going to take in this girl and risk everything we've worked for with the Group just because of what that woman said?"

"That woman is of ancient blood." I said. "We have no reason not to believe her."

"Since when were you religious? You've never put much thought into destiny before. Why have you started now?"

"With what we've just experienced, does it not make you wonder just what the future holds?" I asked. "Doesn't it concern you what this young girl might end up going through if we did nothing to keep her safe?"

"I'm more concerned for you and why you're suddenly so onboard with sheltering a girl just because some woman in a riding cloak told us a fanciful story about her heritage." Avery said. "Why are you really doing this, Luka?"

I knelt by the girl's side again, gently taking her small hand in mine.

"Whether or not there is risk involved, I'm not about to leave this girl alone to face the future alone. She's only a child." I said. "We both promised—"

"No, *you* promised for both of us, Luka." Avery said, his voice heavy with a nearly parental tone. "We have no way of knowing if anything that woman said was true."

I said nothing to defend my actions; I couldn't say anything. I knew that there had been something to what that woman had told us. I thought back to the fateful encounter I had with the girl.

I'd seen her as she limped down the rubbish-filled streets of the Outer District. She was covered in ash and soot, and she was panting like she'd been running a long way. She had been dragging something behind her, something large and black. I thought that she'd been dragging a blanket behind her, but when she'd gotten closer, I realized it wasn't a blanket at all.

It was a large wing with black feathers soaked with blood.

Her magenta-pink eyes had been glowing in the dark of the street, and they were tired and devoid of the innocent spark that usually shone in a child's eyes.

"Luka—"

"If you won't keep the promise to that woman," I said, looking at him, "will you at least promise *me* that you'll protect her? Please, Avery?"

Avery ran a hand through his sandy blonde hair with a sigh, and he gave a reluctant nod.

"I promise."

I breathed a sigh of relief; I knew I could trust his word.

He was my partner, after all.

My *animae nexum*.

The girl's hand flinched, and I turned back to the couch. She was stirring from her sleep. Her eyes opened halfway to reveal those magenta-pink hues, and she turned her head to look at me. Had she the strength, I'm sure she would have jumped away from me. She must have known that she was still weak, and so she settled for just staring at me. Her brow furrowed as she looked at me, gauging whether or not I was a threat.

Very astute survival instincts for such a young girl.

"You're alright." I said with a soft smile. "I found you in the street, and I brought you to my home. My name is Luka, Luka Coltt."

She just stared at me. I could only imagine what she was thinking about me; with survival instincts like hers, she also had a mind to rival that of an adult.

She took a deep breath and sat up, pushing my hand away when I was trying to help her. She turned to look at the both of us.

"Xyla..." She said, her voice raspy from her long sleep. "My name... is Xyla..."

1

ESCAPE TO THE PAST

Phoenix

I GRITTED MY TEETH in pain as Kaylen Crescent — Lexy's eighteen-year-old brother — treated my healing ribs. My torso was covered in bruises from where I'd been kicked by the black ops agents that we'd run into when we'd been about to escape. It was a little hard to breathe, but I gritted my teeth to bear it.

"Sorry, Alpha." He whispered.

"I'm not your Alpha, Kaylen." I said.

"No offense, but you *are* our Alpha." The other shifter — the sixteen-year-old brother of Kaylen named Gerimy — said from the front seat.

I sighed as Kaylen continued to treat my wounds. He was trying hard not to berate his brother for talking back to a superior; the look on his face told me that much.

"What are you two even doing here?" I asked, looking between the two brothers. "Why did you follow us? You should have been helping with the evacuation of the civilians."

"Lexy told us to make sure you and the woman made it out of the Den." Gerimy answered. "She said to look after you and the new Luna."

"She told us to consider it an order." Kaylen added.

I wish I'd been drinking, because if I had been, I wouldn't have suffered the indecency of choking on my tongue. I immediately looked at Xyla in the driver's seat; her eyes were forward, not even looking at me in the rearview mirror.

I could tell that she was on edge because of the brothers' words, but she wasn't letting her irritation show.

"Phoenix, who even are these two?" She asked, her magenta-pink eyes flitting to the mirror to look at me for a second before looking back at the road.

Okay, maybe she wasn't hiding her irritation as much as I thought was.

"They're Lexy's younger brothers." I explained. "Kaylen and Gerimy Crescent."

"That woman sent her kid brothers to help us?"

"We are *not* kids." Gerimy said, his tone in a clear snarl as he glared at her. "We are both grown-ass adults."

I sighed and leaned my head back against the window; Gerimy's stubbornness was going to clash with Xyla, given she was as stubborn as any adolescent wolf-shifter.

"Gerimy, behave yourself." Kaylen said, stopping his work to look at his brother. "Be respectful of our Luna."

"Kaylen—" I started.

"I'm only doing this because Lex asked us to." Gerimy bit back at his brother. "I don't like that bastard any more than she does, but why are we risking our lives and the lives of the Pack for some—"

"Watch your tongue, Gerimy." Kaylen growled.

Just as the brothers were about to snarl at each other, Xyla stomped on the brakes, nearly flinging us from our seats. I grunted as I braced myself against the back of the front passenger seat. She turned in her seat and looked at us; I'm not sure why she was including me in her glare.

"Shut the fuck up, all of you!" She shouted, her teeth bared in a snarl. "I am trying to drive, and your bickering is not helping my concentration!"

The brothers flinched and shrank back in their seats; I'd only ever seen them react that way when Lexy was scolding him. She sighed and turned back around, rubbing her forehead.

"We need a plan." She said after she regained her composure, letting her hands slip from the steering wheel. "We need a place to lie low for a while."

"I agree." Kaylen said as he focused on my ribs again. "We're lucky that the abuse you received did not make these wounds worse, but your ribs will be sore for a while."

"I have a place we can stay in the city." She said. "With Brine dead, no one else should know about it."

"No, that won't work." I said with a wince as I sat up a little. "Cathedral had their hands all over this. They'll know about the house."

"Well, the 'hands all over' comment sounded slightly inappropriate." Gerimy muttered as he crossed his arms and fell back against the seat.

"The kid's irrelevant comment aside," Xyla said, "that house isn't what I'm talking about. There *is* another place we can stay."

She straightened in her seat and cracked her knuckles before she gripped the steering wheel; I wasn't sure why, but the gesture made it seem like she was going to sock Gerimy in the jaw if he said anything else.

Luckily, the youngest Crescent brother kept his mouth shut, and Xyla drove again. I was waiting for her to reveal our destination, but she didn't say a word; it was clear that she wouldn't tell us.

"Uh... Luna—" Kaylen addressed.

"Enough." She said with a tired sigh. "Don't... call me Luna... just... continue treating Phoenix's wounds, please..."

Kaylen frowned and then looked at me, silently asking me what to do. I shrugged; well, as well as I could with a bruised torso.

"Yes, ma'am." Kaylen answered as he went back to his work.

The vehicle's cab was quiet, and it suddenly got quieter when I'd realized that Xyla was no longer calling me "agent", "tracker", or "lapdog": she'd actually called me by name.

How long had she been actually calling me by my name when talking to me?

With everything that happened in the month prior, we'd rarely spoken given that I was being treated for my injuries and rehabilitated from the battle in the Pit; this was the first time that we'd really spent time together.

Though, I doubt that being on the run with another could count as "spending time with each other."

I stared at the back of her head as she drove, her long hair being more white than it was black; she'd not been able to dye her hair during our stay at the Den, so now it was turning back to its original pristine hue.

To me, it was beautiful.

We'd driven the perimeter that separated Mid-City from the Outskirts, and we found ourselves in the Historical District; the architecture belonged to that of the New Era, a piece of the original city that had been preserved from the modern industrial progress of the rest of Arboriah City. I sort of felt like a little kid on a tour bus, marveling at the mosaic of gray tones that grew darker in some areas and lighter in others. I remember reading about the history of Arboriah City before the First Council renamed it; it had been a time of much worse persecution and discrimination than in the current age, but

Arboriah Lux and the return of the Gods' Tree had put aside the classes that separated the people and strove for unification and equality.

"Where are we?" Kaylen asked, sharing my wonderment.

"Welcome to Obsiditourma." Xyla said. "The *original* city of our age's predecessors."

She pulled the vehicle into an alley and turned off the engine. She got out and stretched so nonchalantly. Her lack of wonder astonished me, but considering that she was our guide in this medieval hideout; I imagined that the novelty had worn off for her.

Kaylen helped me out of the backseat, and I looked at Xyla with wide eyes.

"I didn't know that this place was part of the City." I said.

"Yeah, and you wouldn't." She said. "Cathedral only focuses on the *newer* parts of the city. They don't care about the history of where we came from."

She turned and climbed creaky old stairs up to a door. She opened the door and turned to the three of us as we just stared at the building she'd brought us to. She huffed and motioned for us to follow.

"Well, come on." She said. "Phoenix needs a proper bed to rest and recover."

Kaylen and Gerimy helped me up the stairs, and Xyla led us into an apartment living space. There was a mix of antiquated furniture and broken appliances that had been repaired several times. The room was a blend of history and modern renovation. It looked like a museum exhibit.

An exhibit that had currently been lived in.

Xyla came through a door with some thick blankets and pillows.

"The apartment is small, so you guys are going to end up sharing the living room." She said as she draped a blanket and pillow over the arm of an incredibly worn couch. "I'll see what I can do about food. There should be some canned goods in the cellar."

I slowly reclined on the couch and looked at our host.

"What is this place?" I asked, trying to focus on her rather than on my own sore body. "How do you know of it?"

She paused as I addressed her. She took a deep breath and then let her head drop before she turned to look at me.

"This is the overhead apartment where Mariam lived, the mother of Lady Luxia and Esilas Solani." She answered. "And... this is where I lived when I left the Black Wing Group to investigate the Rising and find my sister."

She darted out of the room before any of us could ask any more questions, and I let out a sigh, leaning my head back against the armrest.

"That woman is too mysterious for my liking." Gerimy muttered as he crossed his arms. "Can we really trust her?"

"She brought us to the one place she went to when she went off grid." I said, looking at the two of them. "I trust her, so please do the same."

Gerimy grimaced, but relented. Kaylen cleared his throat and then knelt beside the couch.

"What should we do about the Den?" He asked. "We left—"

"I know, Kay." I sighed as I laid my forearm over my eyes. "For now, we can't really do anything. We can't risk ourselves just after we made our escape."

I knew why Kaylen was asking, and it just wasn't because of Lexy still being at the Den; his mate was there, and considering the girl's shy nature, I could only imagine how nervous he was for her. I looked at him and grasped his shoulder, giving it a reassuring squeeze.

"Don't worry." I said. "We will return to the Den, Kaylen."

Eventually.

He nodded and then stood up. He and Gerimy decided to look around while I rested; I envied that, considering that we were literally hiding in history. This was where our ancestor, Esilas Solani, was born, where the origin of wolf-shifters began.

This was where Esilas Solani's mother lived, the tavern where she first met Ailgraym Solani.

Where Esilas and Lady Luxia were born before being separated from each other.

I wanted so much to explore, to see the tavern below, but my bruised ribs made it hard for me to move or even breathe without feeling pain.

'I'll satisfy that curiosity later,' I thought, 'when I don't feel so sore.'

Xyla returned with a small basket of canned goods. She said nothing as she warmed each can separately on a hotplate.

No one said anything, actually; I don't think anyone really knew what to say.

All I could do was think about the Den and the state we'd left it in; I feared for Lexy and the others that fought against Joshuah's tyranny because of me.

How many had died?

How many had been taken as prisoners of war?

How many had escaped?

'I should have asked Lex what her plan was before we escaped.' I scolded myself for my lack of foresight.

The smell of beef paste wafted in front of my nose, pulling me from my thoughts. I looked up to see Xyla holding a can of beef paste and tomato sauce out for me to take.

"Phoenix, you need to eat." She said. "Get your strength back."

I took the can from her, my fingertips brushing against her knuckles. The touch was enough to send a shock through my veins; it must have affected her, too, because her pale cheek dusted with color.

The connection didn't last long; she pulled away and went to sit at a desk in the room's corner.

She didn't want to feel the Pull; I could tell from how she acted, and I couldn't blame her for that, not after what she'd told me.

'Every time she feels a connection with someone, that person ends up leaving her, whether it be tragic death or cruel abandonment.'

The thought made my heart ache for her and what she'd been through; I didn't want her to be alone.

But I couldn't push her.

Nothing good would come from me forcing the Bond on her. It wasn't right to push on her.

So, I wouldn't do anything to make her feel like a choice was being forced on her.

I'd leave it to her to decide what she wanted and when she wanted it.

Xyla disappeared after eating, leaving the three of us in the larger living area. Kaylen and Gerimy had stayed up for a while, keeping to themselves before falling asleep. I was still awake as well into the night, listening to the soft snoring of the Crescent brothers.

I imagined they needed the rest because they had shifted to protect me and Xyla, to save us from Brine.

But I was restless.

I was worried about Lexy and those who'd fought for our escape, and I was thinking about this place that Xyla had brought us to.

This was where Xyla went after she left the Black Wing Group; I wanted to know what her life was like between her leaving and the first time we met. And the more I wondered about that, the more my curiosity grew, making me even more restless.

"Fuck." I muttered.

I eased up from where I was lying on the couch, hissing through clenched teeth as I held my side, and went to look around the tavern apartment.

There were only a few rooms is that apartment, one larger room that was the kitchen and living area and two smaller bedrooms. There was one bedroom with a closed door; if I had to guess, it was Xyla's room. The door to the room was slightly ajar with light flooding into the hall. I pushed the door open to see a corkboard with a map of printed articles that went back twenty-six years.

Disappearances of children with their families having been murdered.

The papers reported the horror and mystery of the series of crimes, how local law enforcement made no headway in the case. The people were outraged that their children hadn't been found, but even with the public outcry, officials of Cathedral did nothing.

"People looked for them for years." I turned to find Xyla, leaning against the door-frame. "Even after the time frame for their survival had long since passed."

She walked over to the board and looked at the information she'd collected.

"But... what does this have to do with why you left?" I asked. "I thought you left the Group to look for your sister."

She nodded.

"I'd asked around some contacts of mine in the city's underground." She said. "They're the ones that told me about Seraphim and connection with the missing children cases from the time around the orphanage fire."

Xyla pointed to a timeline she'd made of the events, gesturing to one article in particular. The headline read "Abductions and Murder Spree Come To A Stop: Children's Bodies Still Not Found."

"The abductions all stopped on the twenty-seventh of June." She said. "Just a few days before the fire at Lady Luxia's House."

I tried to wrap my head around the new information; the dates coincided with the end of the experiments in the file that Graeves had given me.

"Before I helped you escape," I said, "I went to the Archives Division to look into Seraphim... and I was given a file."

She turned to me with a raised eyebrow; I continued to speak as she just looked at me.

"The file... it had reports for experiments that they did on children, sets of twins." I said, smearing a hand down my face. "The project was called Seraphim. It was clear that they didn't know what they were looking for. According to this information, the experiments ended around the same time as the abductions, just before the orphanage fire."

Xyla turned to face me completely, her brow furrowed in contemplation.

"Cathedral was behind all of it... but why?" She asked. "Why would they be looking for whatever they were looking for in children?"

I shook my head, and then an idea came to mind.

"I think... I might know someone who could give us the answer." I said, looking at her. "The one who gave me the file might have some more answers."

"You want to see your man inside Cathedral?" She asked, and her eyes narrowed with scrutiny. "How do you know he won't betray us?"

"Because he wouldn't have given me the file if he was going to betray me."

Xyla scoffed and gave a sigh, running her hand through graying hair. She closed her eyes as if she was weighing the options. After a while, she let out a breath, and she looked at me.

"Alright." She said. "Now, before we actually go to see this mystery man, please tell me you actually have a plan here."

I rolled my eyes and turned on my heel, though it was a slow motion considering the pain.

"I've worked with the man for years." I said. "I'm pretty sure his routine hasn't changed at all."

I didn't tell her I prayed he would even see us. I wasn't sure if he'd want to see me after I'd been so impulsive with the information he'd given me.

There was also the worry that he was under surveillance because of our meeting in the Archives Division; I wasn't sure if the director knew about our conversation, but I wouldn't put it past him.

But still...

Xyla and I both needed answers, and Old Man Graeves was the only one that could provide them.

2

PASSAGES LONG FORGOTTEN

Jaye

I SUBMITTED MY REPORT and paperwork for my not-so-clandestine observation of the Den, and I leaned back in my chair, smearing my hand down my face.

Fuck, what had I done?

I was on thin ice, and it was a very precarious position.

I was under suspicion for being on an impromptu recon mission without my supervisor's approval. Missions like that are supposed to be with a partner, so two people corroborate the information gained during said mission.

I'd broken the rules, so I was being watched closely; the guy watching me wasn't exactly a top class spy

But being watched meant that I couldn't return to the Den for Lexy.

And with the Den being out of Cathedral's jurisdiction anyway, I couldn't act without being invited or requesting permission.

'With this latest incident, Joshuah Bryte won't grant any request for help.' I thought. 'The Den is on total lockdown.'

I was worried about Lexy; the Bond we had kept pulling at my chest, trying to bring me back to her, back to the question that had been raised from the whispering winds near the Gods' Tree in the Den.

"Worry not for your love or your bloodline, descendant of Passor. They will be safe."

The words of that ethereal woman echoed once again in my ears, and my gut was telling me that my tenfold worry was sound.

'Could it be... that she's—?'

I pinched the bridge of my nose, squeezing my eyes so tightly shut that I could see stars behind my eyelids. I hated to go about my day like nothing was wrong, but with eyes watching my every move, I couldn't act.

"Your name is Jaye Hazelle, yes?"

My head snapped up, and I saw an elderly man with graying red hair. I fought to not raise my eyebrow at the man's appearance.

Was he an agent, or was he a visitor?

And if he was a visitor, why was he seeing me?

"Agent?"

I blinked and nodded, straightening myself in my seat.

"Uh, yeah." I said, clearing my throat. "I'm Jaye Hazelle, Investigator."

The man stood tall—well, as tall as he could—and he held out his hand.

"My name is Oliver Graeves, Senior Specialist in the Archives Division." He introduced himself.

I stood from my desk chair and shook his hand.

"A pleasure to meet you, sir." I said, trying not to show my apprehension. "What brings you to the Investigation Division?" I asked him.

"I... have some questions about a certain tracker we both know." He said, sitting in the chair beside my desk.

I raised an eyebrow and sat down in my desk chair again. I leaned back as I looked at him.

"And... what tracker would that be?" I asked, still cautious about who he was; I didn't know if he was testing me or if it was a trap set up by those watching me.

"Don't play coy with me, sonny." He said, leaning against my desk. "I'm talking about Phoenix Bryte."

His voice was just above a whisper, and I fought to not react where any of the director's spies could see.

"You have information on Phoenix?" I asked, reaching for a notepad in my desk drawer. "What can you tell me about his whereabouts?"

"His whereabouts?" He asked.

"Yes." I said as I showed him what I'd written. "His whereabouts."

Mr. Graeves looked at the pad and then at me. I gave him a slight nod.

"I'm being watched."

He cleared his throat.

"Ah, well, I had drinks with him when he came to visit me in the Archives Division." He said. "He wanted advice for something that was on his mind."

I raised an eyebrow and sat the notepad face down.

"He came to see you?" I asked. "Why?"

"You didn't know?" He asked, surprised. "He started out as my assistant in the Archives Division, and after a few months, I recommended him to a friend of mine, the Tracker Division Chief, Lloyd Faulke. That was before he retired, the poor old chap."

I was surprised; I hadn't realized that Phoenix had connections like that.

Lloyd Faulke was a legend in Cathedral; he'd created the Tracker Division as an official department for those specialists that had once been outsourced to a third party company. It had been an inclusive effort for wolf-shifters that had left their packs and were alone in the city, but lately, it was just another level in the Cathedral hierarchy.

Very few cared about racial equality anymore, and I knew Phoenix had dealt with a lot of shit from other Investigators and other agents in the organization.

I cleared my throat and focused back on the conversation at hand. I needed to speak freely with Mr. Graeves; he knew more about the reason Phoenix did what he did.

True, Phoenix and Xyla were *animae nexum*, but there was more than just instinct that led him to do what he did. I hummed in thought and looked at him to do what he did. I hummed in thought and looked at him.

"Mr. Graeves," I said, tearing the note from my pad and stuffing it in my pocket as I stood up; "will you join me for a bite to eat? I'm feeling rather peckish."

The old man raised an eyebrow at me, and I had to gesture with my eyes off to the side; we were being watched from one of the other desks not too far away from mine. He seemed to understand and stood up as well.

"I could go for a bite to eat." He said. "Where did you have in mind?"

I smiled.

"A favorite place of mine?"

I led him out of the Investigation Division, my tail in hot pursuit, but as soon as Mr. Graeves and I were alone in the elevator, and a certain that my tail had seen what floor we were going to, I opened the doors again and looked at him.

"Come on. I've got another way where we can get out." I said.

The older man chuckled.

"As do I." He said. "I know of all the twists and turns in this old building."

Before I could even ask, he pressed the button for the basement where the Archives Division was. The doors closed, and I looked at him as he watched as the numbers counted down.

The old man seemed rather satisfied with himself, a proud little on his face.

Ding!

The doors opened to a rather dour hallway with flickering lights against chipped and flaking walls, and Mr. Graeves walked out.

"Come, boy." He said. "The way is through here."

I furrowed my brow and followed the old man into the horror movie hallway.

"I don't understand." I said. "I've seen the plans for this building. There isn't a way out from down here."

"Those plans were drawn up for renovations that have been done over the many years that Cathedral had stood." He said. "However, many, many years ago, this building was known by another name."

He led me to a wall of warm-brown stone, and he pressed on a rather worn brick. When he did, the sound of stone tumblers shifted, and the wall moved, revealing a dark passage. He stepped in and turned on an electric lantern, bathing the path in front of him in white light.

"These are the original paths in the walls of the Royal Estate, and I know these paths like the back of my hand."

He turned and started down the path, and after I pulled myself from my awestruck daze, I quickly followed behind him.

"I don't understand." I said. "How do you know of these tunnels? You're not *that* old."

I realized what I'd said, and I cleared my throat.

"Apologies, sir."

Mr. Graeves chuckled softly.

"No need to apologize." He said. "I may not be as old as this building, but I have had time to learn its secrets."

His experience certainly showed; the old man navigated the tunnels as simply as he would walk down a street. But the question of *how* he knew about the pathways remained unanswered, and I didn't know how to phrase without sounding rude.

Mr. Graeves opened another door with the simple push of a brick, and the tunnel filled with the blinding natural light of the outside. He led me out of Cathedral. I was amazed, and he knew this. The old man had led me through the twists and turns that I'm pretty sure no one else knew existed. He turned off the lantern and put it back inside the tunnel before closing the bit of wall.

"Now, let's eat." Mr. Graves said. "I know a place that might interest you."

I'd completely forgotten that was why I'd let him take point and lead me through secret tunnels. I think that was what finally broke my silence.

"Okay, I *have* to know." I said, looking at him. "I have to know how you knew about those tunnels."

The old man chuckled and pat my shoulders. A smile puffed his wrinkled cheeks, as if he was finding joy in my desperation for answers.

"All in due time, sonny." He said. "Now, your tail'll probably know a yer usual place to eat. Luckily, Solani's ain't the only restaurant in the city."

He walked down the alleyway, and I followed, curious about where he'd led me. To my shock, the architecture of the buildings was nothing like the modern look of the rest of the city.

"The Historical District?" I asked as I turned to him.

"Indeed." He said. "Right now, we're in the Old Academic District. Is one of the few places in this part of the city that remains operational."

I followed the old man as we continued to walk down the streets of our cultural history.

When Arboriah City had expanded, the Council—descendants of Arboriah Lux, Esilas Solani, and Dahliah Passor, among others that made up the First Council—were afraid of losing the past to the rising tides of the future. So, it was decided that parts of the original city would be preserved and maintained as part of the coalition of restoration and remembrance. I remember field trips when I was still in school; learning about the past had always been important to me.

After all, my grandmother's great-grandmother was Dahliah Passor.

Mr. Graeves le us to a small cafe, a true hole-in-the-wall spot, but it gave off an authentic feel. The furniture was all expertly crafted reproductions or beautifully restored antiques. The smell of seasoned, blood-rich meat was potent in the air but not overpowering, mixed with the thick scent of honeyed wine. These were scents typical of taverns in the days of Arboriah Lux.

"This place is a faithful re-establishment of the tavern where Esilas Solani and Lady Luxia were raised by their mother shortly before they were separated." He said. "Though the original tavern is part of the museum path of the Historical District."

I was like a wide-eyed child as we sat down in a corner booth. My eyes traveled around the space, observing every piece of history that had been recreated. My wonderment must have amused Mr. Graeves.

"You didn't know about this place, did ya, sonny?" He asked, a smile clear in his voice.

"No, sir." I said, turning to him. "In all honesty, I've not been to the Historical District since I was in school."

He chuckled softly.

"I'd be surprised if anya ya youngins came to this place, let alone knew about it." He leaned back in his seat with a smile as he spoke. "Rest assured, no one will hear us here as we talk."

I was amazed at his foresight; he'd planned this so that we could *actually* be alone to talk and not worry about anyone eavesdropping. That kind of foresight was a honed skill.

Definitely not something you learn as a file clerk in the Archives Division.

"Who are you exactly?" I asked, leaning forward against the table.

The old man smiled a knowing smile and leaned forward as well. His demeanor changed, and surprisingly, so did his vernacular.

"My name is Oliver Graeves, as I said before," he said with a bemused chuckle, "former agent of Cathedral's black operations unit, a guard of one of this organization's most well-kept secrets."

I found myself leaning in close, as if wanting to be privy to this secret that he was alluding to.

"What secrets?" I asked, a sense of child-like wonder captivating me.

The older man smiled, a chuckle shaking his shoulders as he leaned in.

"I'll tell you." He said. "I tell you and then you must help our mutual friend and that woman he's with."

I furrowed my brow. No one knew Phoenix was with Xyla; how could he have known?

The look in his eye told me what I needed; he knew a lot more than anyone thought he did.

3

NEXT STEP MOVING FORWARD

Xyla

WATER PITTER-PATTERED ON MY face like a heavy rain, warm droplets washing the last remnants of black dye from my hair as I showered. The old tavern had been remodeled with a shower and running water, long before I'd ever taken up residence there. The sector of the Historical District where we were staying was kept as museum exhibits of the original town, but it had also been a residential area before the coalition had moved every exhibit closer to the inner city.

It made the old tavern the perfect place to hide in plain sight.

I turned off the water and wrapped myself in a towel as I stepped out of the shower. Steam hung in the air, illuminated by the soft yellow light of antiquated bulbs. I looked in the tarnished mirror as I wiped the condensation away.

It was strange to see my hair white again; it had been black for so long that I'd almost forgotten that it was naturally so pale. I didn't like how people stared at my white hair or my eyes. I couldn't change my eyes, but I could change my hair. I was ten or eleven years old, and I didn't know anything about dying hair, so I went for the markers. I remember Luka's face when he saw me trying to darken it with those permanent markers, and how he helped me dye my hair black for the first time. That had been a rather fond memory of mine, even though the circumstances leading up to it weren't so great.

Seeing my hair so white again reminded me of that woman in the light blue riding cloak.

The woman with *my* face.

I hated not having answers, but even if I could investigate that woman, I didn't know where to even start.

Gods, what a frustrating dilemma.

And what was worse, I couldn't focus on it with our current situation.

"Don't focus on what you cannot change, Xy." Luka's voice echoed in my head. *"I'm sure that you will find the answers you seek soon enough."*

Luka's words puzzled me; sometimes I wondered if the voice I was hearing in my head was more that just my conscience or my trauma manifesting as my personal ghost that was using his voice.

Was his voice just my brain processing trauma?

Or was I being haunted by the ghost of my adoptive brother?

I shook my head with a sigh; I didn't need another line of inquiry to distract me. I needed to focus on the mission at hand.

But... what *was* the mission, exactly, now that things had gone off the rails?

I wasn't completely on board with Phoenix's plan to see the man he'd learned about Seraphim from. However, I was curious about who this person was.

I got dressed and towel-dried my hair.

"You can't be serious!" That voice belonged to Gerimy, Lexy's brother. "You want to go back?!"

"Not to the Den." Phoenix's voice was calm as he spoke. "Not yet, anyway. We're going to the place I used to live before I got my own place in the city."

"Semantics!" Gerimy exclaimed.

"Calm down." Kaylen said, Lexy's other brother. "Phoenix, are you really sure about this? Why risk it?"

That was an interesting question, and it was an answer that piqued my curiosity.

"Because," Phoenix answered, "the information could help Xyla. We can understand why all this is happening. Everything leads back to Seraphim. Whether we go back to the Den now or later, we can't really act without answers."

My heart skipped a beat in my chest; I hadn't expected that answer, even from Phoenix.

Heat flushed to my cheeks.

Again, he was risking everything for me.

'What the hell is this idiot thinking?!'

"Isn't there a saying that people do crazy things when they're in love?" Luka answered with a question.

I scoffed at the thought and hung up my damp towel. Phoenix wasn't in love with me; he was just someone with a righteous moral code and was far too trusting.

But then I remembered the conversation I'd overheard at the Den.

"Now that they've found each other, Phoenix's claim as Alpha is even more legitimate!"

It had been obvious that Joshuah was in a panic at the thought of us being together, but I didn't understand why; what did my association with Phoenix have to do with him being the more legitimate Alpha?

Kaylen and Gerimy had called me Luna.

What did they know about it?

Perhaps I'd ask Kaylen; he seemed to be a bit more reasonable compared to his younger brother.

I took one last look in the mirror, running my fingers through my damp ribbons of white hair.

I had so many questions that I needed answers to.

I needed to know why these things were happening... and I *hated* not knowing.

Areena

Thwack!

I hit a training dummy with a bo staff so hard that it fell over with a clattering *thud*. I huffed and went to a nearby bench to grab a towel and a water bottle. I'd been training with Hollum's newest regimen for several days; it was perhaps the most meaningless thing to do with my time. I dubbed the towel against my face and across the back of my neck with a sigh.

Xyla and her wolf boy toy had gone off the grid, a setback that my vanguard was *not* happy about; he'd overturned the whole desk in the office during his latest tantrum.

There was something else to he was upset about, but he never spoke of it; every time I'd asked what was wrong, even attempting to show care or concern, he'd just look at me with a forced smile and tell me "not to worry my pretty head."

I hated it, that patronizing tone he'd use whenever he spoke to me; it was like he thought of me as a child.

And I *certainly* was not a child.

I was twenty-six years old, for Gods' sake.

My frustration mounted, and I threw my towel onto the bench. I set up the training dummy again, sourly admitting that this training regimen of Vanguard Hollum's did have some benefits.

'A good way to let out my frustrations, at least.'

I stood with my bo staff, preparing to go through the motions of the regimen again. As I moved to make the first hit, pesky memories that I'd long since tried to purge from the forefront of my mind.

"Sissy, we'll always be together, won't we?"

Thwack!

"Of course, Na-Na. Always together."

Thwack, whoosh, thwack!

"But what if—"

"Look, even if we're separated, we'll always find each other. It's our special twin bond, after all."

Thwack, thwack!"

"Promise, Sissy?"

"Of course, Areena. I'll always find you if you need me."

Thwack, thud!

I'd knocked over the dummy again in my frustration. Memories of that morning before the fire replayed in my mind, ones that I remembered out of painful nostalgia and seething hatred.

I threw my bo staff to the ground and sat against the wall. Tears were threatening to spill over, and I hated those tears so much; all they were was just a reminder of the promise my sister had made and that same promise she'd broken.

'Damn you.' I gritted my teeth at the thoughts of my sister, furiously wiping the tears from my eyes. 'Damn you, *Xyla Coltt*.'

I curled my fingers in my white hair, tugging slightly as I continued to fight the tears. However hard I tried, they continued to build up and trickle from my eyes. My thought forcefully dug up the happier moments in our childhood, and my heart tore itself in pieces once more when I remembered how things once were.

The times we would read about Lady Arboriah Lux and how she'd liberated the city from the villainous Butterfly Killer and his plot to overthrow the Morgenstern Family.

The times my *dear* sister would take the blame for mistakes I'd made.

The times she'd beaten up bullies for throwing mud at us, those kids being two or three years older.

She'd always been the stronger one of the two of us, and she'd always done what was best for me, even if we'd had some stupid fights.

"Damn it…" I muttered, trying not to let my voice crack. "I don't want to remember any of this…"

Footsteps echoed across the spacious training hall, but I didn't look up at who was approaching. I didn't have to; the presence was cool, like a soothing breeze during autumn, and I felt a calloused hand gently pet my head.

This was one of the few times that I didn't hate that gesture of Hollum's; even if rough callouses sometimes snagged strands of my hair, I knew it was during times like this that his gesture was sincere.

"Oh, my darling girl." His smooth voice sounded sweet, and I gently took his hand and put it on my cheek. "Are those pesky memories back?"

I simply nodded, to which he responded with a hum.

"I see." He said, and then he gently turned my face up to his. "I'll ask this again, Areena. Do you want to be rid of those painful memories?"

This wasn't the first time he'd asked me that question; I'd broken down several times before whenever I remembered the heartbreak that followed my sister's actions.

Each time, he'd asked me if I wanted to forget.

And every time he'd asked me, I'd refused; those memories fueled my anger and gave me a reason to continue the charade of "the Fair Lady Priestess" and prepare for the battle where I'd kill Xyla.

But… something in my heart wouldn't let me hate her anymore.

I wanted to find her, to jump into her arms as I cried and feel *her* gentle hands in my hair.

Not Hollum's.

"Areena," Hollum addressed me again, his tone a little more demanding; "do you want—"

"*No.*" I said, gritting my teeth as I pushed his hand away; "I don't want to forget about my sister. I-I want—"

"*You* want to kill your sister." He said, his hazel eyes flickering with glittery specks. "That's what you want, isn't it, *Areena*?"

I clinched my fists and pushed myself up from the floor with a huff.

"Yes, that's what I want." I sighed. "I really wish you would stop asking me if I really want to kill my sister."

Hollum hummed, though it sounded more like a throaty chuckle; what the hell was he so pleased with?

"Of course, dear." He said, his lips curling into a grin. "I was... *just making sure...*"

4

QUESTIONS UPON QUESTIONS

Phoenix

GODS, I WAS STILL sore; it had been a few days since Xyla had brought us to her hideout in the Historical District, and while the bruises had yellowed and had faded away, the pain remained etched into my ribs. It hurt whenever I moved or even breathed, but it was slowly getting better.

"You know, I could have made this supply run myself." Xyla reminded, bringing me out of my thoughts as she picked a can of cheap ravioli from the shelf. "You didn't have to come with me, especially with us being a matched set of criminals in the eyes of Cathedral."

I remembered where we were: the market.

The smell of fresh fruit and vegetables hung in the air like a wafting perfume, and the mouthwatering scent of the butcher cutting meat immediately tugged at my stomach. We were in the canned goods section of the store, and I couldn't help but think that this was the most *normal* scenario despite the reality of our situation.

Xyla had insisted on getting supplies for our journey to see Mr. Graeves, though she didn't know who he was or how long of a journey it was going to be. She'd argued that if there was a time that we'd end up having to lie low somewhere in "enemy territory", then she insisted on being prepared.

It was a sign that she was in survival mode again, but at least she seemed to be focused on the survival of our small group rather that just herself this time around.

"Can you blame me?" I chuckled, which I immediately regretted thanks to the dull ache in my sides. "I've never been to the Historical District before, so I didn't even know that they had a market like this."

She chuckled as she looked at me, putting the canner dinner back on the shelf.

"It's the same as any store they have in the Outskirts or in Mid-City." She said. "The only difference is quality."

"That doesn't change the fact that there's still a mysticism to the Historical District." I said.

"I envy your childlike curiosity." She said as she continued walking down the canned food aisle. "I guess I've lost mine forever."

"Maybe, maybe not." I said. "I remembered you being rather enthralled when you found the Gods' Tree at the Den."

Her pale cheeks tinged with color, and she did her best to hide her smile.

The memory of our conversation under the Tree was perhaps the highlight of our brief stay at the Den; we'd both shared something deeply personal with each other, and I'd thought we'd gotten closer.

But Xyla still kept herself at arm's length from me.

I had to remind myself not to take it personally; she had every right to protect herself from more heartache, given all that she'd been through.

Her sister having gone against her.

Her adoptive brother having died at the hand of a Cathedral cop.

Brine having betrayed her just for going to find her sister.

She probably expected me to betray her at some point, even with all I'd done for her.

I couldn't hold that against her, though; it broke my heart for her, but I couldn't hover, forcing her to feel the Pull.

She had to open herself up to the Bond.

So, I would continue to be patient with her; I owed her that much.

After buying the food we needed, we headed back to the old tavern, but I caught two familiar scents that made me freeze.

Blood tea and aftershave... and old papers and whiskey. The scents were strong, mingled together.

"Old Man Graeves... and Jaye..."

Xyla turned her head back to me, noticing that I'd stopped.

"Phoenix?" She asked, trying to get my attention. "Oi, Phoenix—"

I held up a finger and looked around, trying to find the scent.

"It's a bit stale, but they *were* here."

"Who was here?" She asked, turning to me completely. "Whose scent have you caught?"

I looked at her; her brows were knit together in confusion. I turned my head and caught the scent trail, and I instinctively followed it.

"Phoenix, wait!" She hushed as she hurried after me. "Who are you trying to follow?!"

I didn't answer, following the scent through sparse crowds of people towards an alleyway. The walls were of the same muddy brown stone as the foundations of the Cathedral, and the hair on my neck stood on end.

I didn't realize how close we were to the organization.

"The ancient catacombs?" I muttered.

Old Man Graeves had once told me of the ancient tunnels that were built into the foundation of the Royal Estate, and how they'd been used in dire situations before a former terror of the past had discovered and used them. I ran my fingers along the wall, in awe of how tightly packed the stones were.

"Hah... Phoenix?"

I turned and looked back at the mouth of the alleyway to see Xyla catching her breath. She furrowed a brow at me, and they narrowed a little, though not menacingly.

"Phoenix, *what* is going on?" She asked with a huff.

Had I been running the entire time, and she had to catch up with me?

"An old friend." I said. "He used a secret passageway that many believe to be myth... and he wasn't alone."

"Secret passageway?" She asked. "Phoenix, this isn't some fantasy novel."

She walked over to the wall, putting her hand on a random brick, and she looked at me.

"See?" She said. "It's just a wall. If there was a passageway, you'd think there'd be some sort of trigger—"

Thndt, scraaaaaaape.

A section of the wall moved and both of us flinched and jumped back, watching as a tunnel as black as shadow appeared.

"You were saying?" I asked as I looked at her.

She didn't look at me; her eyes focused on the tunnel. I recognized that look on her face; she was calculating risks, as if she were about to dive into a cave without the correct gear or training.

"Xyla—"

"Do you know where it leads?" She asked, turning to me. "Can you follow the scent?"

Her bold question surprised me; she'd been calm and meticulous in the few days we'd spent in the Historical District. And considering how she seemed to hate Cathedral, I didn't know why she'd even asked.

There were a lot of things I would do for Xyla; hell, I'd risked my life for her already.

But I wasn't about to risk her freedom.

"Xy." I muttered, gently putting my hand on her arm. "We can't risk it."

"You said your friend had opened these tunnels." She said as she turned to look at me. "Can you follow the scent or not?"

Her tone was challenging, as if questioning my loyalty. It was the kind of tone that hurt; I'd thought she'd finally trusted me.

I gritted my teeth and stood in front of her, blocking her view from the tunnel. Her magenta-pink eyes focused on me.

"I *can* track his scent and navigate the tunnels," I said, gently putting my hands on her shoulders; "but I *won't*. I won't risk you getting captured."

The way she was staring at me was between a glare and an analytical stare.

Was she really still suspicious of me?

She then let out a sigh and hung her head. Her tense shoulders drooped in defeat.

"You're right..." she muttered. "I... apologize..."

She forced the apology from her throat, and the defeat in her voice made me feel guilty; following the scent would have inevitably led us to my friend, but it came with the risk of getting caught.

We knew nothing about those tunnels, and we didn't know who else had access to them.

I touched my forehead to hers, slowly trailing my hands up to the nape of her sorry, Xy." I whispered. "You'll get the answers you seek. I promise."

She didn't answer me; she just stared at the ground, her fingers curled into her palms. She was frustrated with the situation, and I understood that feeling all too well. I felt like I needed to say something, but every thought I had on the matter would only make things worse.

The silence must have gotten to her, because she let out a sigh as she closed her eyes. She brushed my hands away and stepped back to turn on her heel.

"We should get back." She said, picking up the shopping backs of canned goods. "Kaylen and Gerimy are probably worried, wondering where their leader is."

Ouch.

She probably hadn't meant to, but she sounded condescending.

I let out a sigh, and I looked back at the opening to the tunnel. The stones had scraped closed, returning to the dead end it had been before, and my brow furrowed all the more.

'How do Jaye and Mr. Graeves know each other?' I wondered. 'And why were they using the tunnels to get out of Cathedral?'

I was worried about Jaye and the predicament that I'd left him in. In so many ways, I wished I could apologize to him. And I certainly wanted to, but with how things were now, I couldn't do anything.

I turned back and followed Xyla back to the old tavern, my thoughts reeling with confusion and questions that I probably would never get the answers to.

5

THE TRIALS OF LEXISHIRA, PART ONE

Lexy

THE AIR OF THE basement was stale, filled with the sounds of coughs, wheezes, and the sickening metallic scent of blood. After the uprising, the basement of the Alpha House was turned into a makeshift dungeon to hold those of us who'd been captured by Joshuah's combined troops, but there had been something to happen during the uprising that no one had expected.

Most of the members of the Black Wing Group had fought *with* us against the Cathedral soldiers that Joshuah had gained instead of working with the larger group; a wolf-shifter with sandy blonde hair had led the Group on our side of the rebellion.

He had thankfully gotten many of the children, elderly and rebels away from the Den when our defensive line fell; Celia had been among them, thank the Gods' Tree.

She would have hopefully led them to the Sanctuary; even with Joshuah's knowledge of it, he didn't know where it was, precisely.

'Please, Gods.' I prayed. 'Keep everyone safe. Keep us alive.'

Once again, nausea churned in my stomach as I shifted, and I fought the urge to vomit.

"Miss Lexy? Are you alright?" The older shifter that was next to me—one of the Group members that had been captured; his name was Thomas, I believe—spoke as he cradled his broken arm.

"I'm fine, Thomas." I said, trying not to retch. "It's just... the smell is getting to me..."

"But you're a doctor." He said, an eyebrow raised.

After a moment, he gave a hum, as if understanding why I was sick. He shifted a little closer in an attempt to keep our conversation private.

"How far along are you?" He whispered.

I willed my stomach to calm down, and I sighed, resting my head against the rough concrete wall beside us.

"I'm not sure." I said, truthfully. "Few weeks... maybe a little over a month?"

"And yet, you still instigated the rebellion?" He asked.

I nodded without a word, which seemed to confuse him all the more.

"But why?"

It was my turn to raise an eyebrow at his words.

"Is it not obvious?" I asked. "Because he needs to be stopped. Joshuah has wanted nothing but power since he was a child. Phoenix was a better leader than he ever will be."

Click.

The locked door at the top of the stairs opened, creaking on squeaky hinges. The sound silenced any murmuring or hushed sounds of suffering.

Thunk, creak.

Thunk, creak.

Slow footsteps descended the staircase, each pause putting the surrounding captives more and more on edge.

I did my best to keep calm as I felt my stomach churning again; I knew who was coming down those steps.

"Gods, it's repulsive down here." Joshuah said, covering his nose. "It smells like blood, shit, and piss."

He sounded like he was disgusted, but it was more than that; he was mocking us, rubbing our noses in the mess.

I narrowed my eyes. A dog treating captive wolves like scolded pups...

It was rather ironic.

Joshuah had sunk to a new level of pitiful, so pitiful that I didn't even consider him a shifter.

No, he was a dirty rat with a superiority complex.

I gritted my teeth, and I choked on the vomit that rose to my throat. I couldn't keep it down this time, and I turned my head to the side to retch. It forced itself up from my stomach, leaving a disgustingly shuddering taste in my mouth as it splattered on the floor.

"Ah, there's my lovely mate." Joshuah said. "Showing more signs of pregnancy, my beloved *Lexishira*?"

I groaned, spitting the taste out before looking at him. He had that arrogant smirk on his crooked lips. He snapped his fingers and two lackeys—they were two of the wolf-shifters that had stayed on his side out of fear—walked over to me. I gritted my teeth, my back flat against the wall as they came closer.

I hated how trapped I felt.

Rough hands grabbed my arms and yanked me from the ground, and Thomas fought to get up from where he'd been sitting.

"Hey, don't manhandle her!"

"Oh shut it, you stray!" one lackey said as he kicked him back.

"Oi, he's already got a broken arm that needs to be set!" I growled at them. "Leave him alone!"

"Shut it, bitch!"

"Now, now, boys." Joshuah said as he stepped forward, reaching into his jacket. "Be gentle with my wife. She's carrying my child, after all."

Nausea churned in my stomach again as he said those words. I wanted to tell him he was wrong, that he couldn't breed a hooker with his limp dick.

But I forced my tongue to stay behind my teeth; I couldn't put myself any more at risk, not with my *animae nexum*'s baby in my belly.

I couldn't risk Jaye being found out, either.

"You, however," he said, pulling out a gun, "are of no use to me."

Before I could even comprehend what he was doing, the close quarters of the basement reverberated with the loud bang of a gunshot.

My ears were ringing as blood splattered across the concrete wall, and the nausea grew worse in my belly. The other prisoners were trying not to make a sound, fearing that doing so would provoke the madman to shoot again.

Joshuah put his gun away, and he turned to me with a menacing grin. He walked past me, and I was pushed into walking up the stairs. Hot tears welled in my eyes as I forced myself to look away from the fresh corpse of the man who had been so kind to me in the days since our imprisonment.

'Thomas... I am so sorry...'

The air of the Alpha House was just as stale to me as it had been in the basement; all the life, even the forced atmosphere before the rebellion, had been sucked out of everything. Colors seemed more dull, and it was cold.

Freezing cold.

I fought a shudder as one of my "escorts" pushed me into one of the residential rooms. While the room had many of the comforts that someone in my condition needed—a proper bed and a complete bathroom—I knew what this was.

This was just another prison cell, and it was mine.

"Now that you're not surrounded by sickness and death," Joshuah sneered, "*our* baby can grow with the proper care."

His words made me feel sick to my stomach again; he *knew* the baby wasn't his, but he was using it to legitimize his fragile control over the Pack.

He was grasping at straws, and he knew it; I could see that he was practically losing his sanity over it.

He caressed my cheeks with his hands, and my nausea grew worse; his touch felt like slime against my skin. Even though I was doing my best to not show how disgusted I was, it was clear that Joshuah was pleased with it. His lips curled into a sickening smirk as he leaned in.

"All I need is the child." He whispered, his breath fanning against my cheeks. "After he's born, you won't ever see him again. And when your *beloved* partner comes for you, I'll kill him in front of you. Or maybe it'll be the other way around. I've not decided yet."

His hands wrapped around my throat, not squeezing tight, but enough to clarify that he was calling the shots.

"If you weren't carrying that baby in your belly, I'd kill you just for embarrassing me as you have." He growled.

All I could do was narrow my eyes at him as he spouted confirmation of his fragile ego. Joshuah let go of my neck and turned on his heel.

He left me alone in that room, and after a moment, I felt so sick to my stomach that I ran to the bathroom. I wasn't sure if it was because of the baby or the fact that Joshuah's touch was just so nauseating now that I'd found my *animae nexum*.

Thinking about Jaye caused my chest to tighten.

I missed him.

I needed him there with me, or I needed to be wherever he was.

I wiped the bile from my mouth, my tears from my retching turning to tears of heartache.

'Jaye...'

6

STARTING TOWARDS THE UNKNOWN

Xyla

AFTER A FEW WEEKS of preparation and waiting for Phoenix to recover—in truth, he'd already healed from the beatings he'd received at the hands of the agents; he and the two brothers had spent a better part of their time arguing about the best course of action—it was finally time for us to make the journey to his friend.

"With all the supplies we have, why aren't we taking the truck?" Kaylen asked.

"We're not taking everything." I reminded him. "This place is a safe house of sorts. It needs to be kept stocked in case anyone needs to hide away for a while."

It was a very thin reason to give, but it was part of the truth; the truck could easily be recognized, and no one was that good-hearted to not be a snitch.

But, in reality, I didn't want to say goodbye to that place forever; it was the place where Esilas Solani's story started before he met Arboriah Lux.

I stepped outside to get some air, and I leaned against the wall of the tavern. I ran my hand through my hair with a sigh. I looked back at the stairs that led to the overhead apartment.

"There's not a reason for you to not come back, Xy." Luka's voice spoke again, which was both a comfort and a worry. *"You can always come back, even for a visit."*

I still didn't know what his voice was, and the most realistic explanation wasn't as much as a comfort as the other.

Whether or not he was a ghost, I still answered him.

'I know... but this place still feels so much like home to me.' I thought. 'Even more so than with the Group...'

"Even with Avery?"

Admittedly, I did miss Avery; he was the closest thing to family I had left, given the Areena was trying to kill me now.

'No... I do miss him...' I said. 'You and he practically raised me. You both became my fathers.'

Luka raised me like I was his daughter, but he treated me like his sister. It had been awkward for Avery, but he did right by me.

It was those connections that I treasured.

'I miss you both.'

"You still have one of us, Xy." Luka said, his voice sounding melancholic.

It was times like that when his voice seemed real; Luka and Avery were *animae nexum*, and their bond had been strong. Avery had taken Luka's death harder than I had, hardly eating or leaving their shared bedroom after his funeral.

At the thought of *animae nexum*, my thoughts drifted to Phoenix and the conversation I'd overheard at the Den. Joshuah had told Areena and Brine that Phoenix was my *animae nexum*.

The memory made blood flush to my cheeks, and even though the very thought of it seemed ridiculous to me, it made my heart skip a beat all the same.

There was a certain pull I felt for the former Tracker, but it made me as uneasy as it did ecstatic; I wanted nothing more than to embrace the connection, but fear ate away at me.

Fear of losing another person I held dear.

"It's okay to let yourself love another person again, Xyla." Luka's words weren't as comforting as he probably meant them to be. *"Whether it's familial, or it's romantic."*

I didn't want to lose anyone else; Luka's death made me resolve to keep everyone at arm's length, and even the hope I'd felt when I realized Areena was alive was extinguished when I realized how far gone she was.

"You can't keep your heart locked away forever." He spoke, trying to reason with the fear that I was grappling with. *"Doing so will only leave you with regrets."*

I let out a sigh as I rubbed my eyes, resting the back of my head against the wall again. I looked up at the pale blue sky, rays of the white sun shining on the tops of the buildings.

'Regrets...'

Well, I had plenty of those already.

"Xy?"

I nearly jumped at the nickname, and I turned my head to see Phoenix standing there. How long had he been standing there?

"What?" I asked, though I probably sounded a bit more agitated than I really was.

"Kaylen and Gerimy are ready to go." He said. "And we need to go if we're going to the other side of the city before tomorrow."

Oh, right. There was also that little detail.

The "friend" that Phoenix wanted to see was on the other side of the city... and we were traveling on foot.

"Yeah, fine." I said, pushing off the wall and grabbing my backpack, which had most of my notes and some food. "Lead the way, tracker."

Again, the unnecessary bite of agitation where I hadn't meant it.

Phoenix's brow twitched a little; the glisten in his eye reflected hurt, and it made me hurt as well.

I hated I didn't have my feelings sorted, but I hated I seemed so at war with myself over it.

"Sorry." I apologized. "That was uncalled for."

"You don't have to apologize." He said, a sigh clear in his voice. "You're in survival mode... I've learned to see whether the switch has flipped."

I blinked at his words, feeling rather exposed; was I really that easy to read?

Before I could say anything else, he just gave me a somber smile.

"You've always acted for your own survival. It's nothing new." He said as he stood in front of me, leaning close to me; I didn't pull away when he touched his forehead to mine. "I know it will take time... but I hope you'll let me in... let me be the one to watch your back..."

My chest tightened at his words, and I wanted to let him in, to let him handle the burden I carry. But before I could even say anything, he pressed his lips to my forehead and pulled away, a flush of pink coloring on his cheeks.

I could only imagine how red mine were, even with my restraint.

Phoenix smiled at me, the somber curve still there that mixed with relief.

"Well, let's get going, shall we?"

There was so much I wanted to tell him at that moment, but I didn't know where to start. He turned and walked away, and Kaylen and Gerimy appeared from around the corner.

The moment was gone, and with it, the words I wanted to say.

I took a deep breath, easing the tightness in my chest as I put my backpack over my shoulder. I kept my words to myself as I followed Phoenix and the two brothers.

It had taken the whole day to traverse the city inconspicuously. I had to keep my hood up to hide my hair, which was already stuffed into the collar of my shirt, and we had to avoid public areas where Cathedral's camera system could identify us. By the time night had fallen, we'd made our way to a low-wage housing building; it was one of the many projects that the City Council had built for citizens who weren't given any pay.

Gerimy looked at the building and then at Phoenix.

"What's this shit hole?"

His brother met with a smack to the back of his head because of the unfiltered question.

"Low-wage housing." I answered with a sigh. "It's a place for less fortunate households and city employees, which means that most of the residents are either Bottom Rung Cathedral agents or backroom Council Hall employees."

"Well, you're not wrong." Phoenix said as he started towards the door. "There aren't many Cathedral agents that live here... actually, hardly anyone lives here."

"So, what are we doing here?" I asked.

"Because this is where my friend lives." He answered as he opened the door for us. "He's one of the few residents that live here."

The interior was grimy, but I expected very little from a building that was meant for low-income households. The lights flickered unceremoniously, and the air was stale with the odor of mildew and dust. The wallpaper was flaking off the walls in some place and there were air bubbles in others.

The building was in such neglect that there was a visible layer of dust on the "out of order" sign that was taped to the elevator.

"This way." Phoenix said as he climbed the stairs. "He lives on the third floor, room twelve."

The stairs creaked as we climbed them to the designated floor, and the air became thick with anxiety with every step; I knew it wasn't from Phoenix, considering he'd obviously been there before.

'Makes sense that Kaylen and Gerimy are on edge.' I hummed in thought. 'Phoenix is being rather cryptic, which makes their jobs harder."

When we reached the third floor, the staleness of the air had grown thicker, and a humid musk hung in the air like shower steam. It felt like it was getting harder to breathe, but I continued to follow Phoenix down the dimly lit hallway. I read the apartment numbers as we walked, side-stepping crumpled papers and bits of rubbish on the floor.

C9.

C10.

C11.

And then we stopped outside apartment C12.

Phoenix spent a few moments staring at the door; what was he thinking?

Why did he suddenly look so nervous?

His fingers tightened into his palms, and he seemed to swallow his doubts as he reached out to knock on the door.

Knock, knock, knock.

Those knocks reverberated through the hall, and I found myself holding my breath as we waited for the door to open. After a few moments, there was a grumbling from the other side.

"Ya damn cretins!" The voice of an older man growled. "I oughta call juvenile services on yer asses!"

I was bewildered, not so much at the older man's words, but more of the fact that Phoenix was laughing with relief.

Had he expected this?

"Sorry, sir." He said. "I'm afraid that I—or rather, *we*—have nowhere else to go."

Silence.

After a few moments, the lock turned, and the door opened a crack, and it opened to reveal an older man with curly gray-red hair and bushy eyebrows.

"Phoenix? I never thought I'd see you back here, lad."

My eyes narrowed a little at his change in vocabulary; he seemed to speak more properly than when he'd yelled.

"Yeah, sorry to impose." Phoenix said. "I—*We* need your help."

The man looked at me, and there was a flash of familiarity in his eyes. My brows knit in confusion.

What was that look for?

"Yes." He said, his voice almost breathy. "Yes, I can see that."

I looked at Phoenix.

"Who is this guy?"

He looked at me and the brothers, and he offered a rather relieved smile.

"Everyone, this is my friend and my mentor." He said, turning back to the old man. "This is Oliver Graeves."

7

MR. GRAEVES

Xyla

THE OLD MAN, MR. Graeves, had little in his apartment, but he certainly had a lot of photographs on his wall. It reminded me a lot of Luka and the photographs he kept in our old house. I noticed several of them were of a younger Mr. Graeves and a group of men. There were some of him and Phoenix, too, and it caught me a bit off guard; the former tracker's hair was longer, reaching down to the top of his shoulders, sort of how it was now. His eyes held sorrow and guilt.

'Must have been not long after he left the Pack.' I deduced. 'When his wife was killed by his own brother.'

That revelation still left an unpleasant taste in my mouth; it was only the surface of the mystery surrounding everything. I hoped that this Mr. Graeves could answer the questions we had.

"You're the Mesmer I've heard so much about."

My attention snapped back to the old man as he offered a drink to me. I took the cup from him—it was filled with water—and I took a sip.

"Yes, sir." I said, looking at him. "What has Phoenix told you?"

"Oh, *he's* not told me anything." He said as he chuckled heartily. "I've heard about you from another agent. Phoenix's partner, actually."

I looked at Phoenix as he cleared his throat, fidgeting in the place where he was sitting; was that the other scent he'd caught at the market that day?

"Although, with everything I discussed with that Investigator and with Phoenix, it doesn't surprise me you were the one who mentioned Seraphim." The old man said. "You certainly have a way of hyper-focusing. You let nothing go if it bothers you."

I looked at him with a raised eyebrow; how did he know about that?

What else did he know about Seraphim?

How did he know anything about *me*?

I must have had a skeptical look on my face because his cheeks rose with a smile that reached his kind eyes—the kind of smile that reminded me of Luka.

"Don't you worry, dear girl." He said, gently taking my hand in his and giving it a soft pat. "I have no intention or reason to turn you over to Cathedral."

My brow furrowed at his words.

"But why?" I asked. "You don't even know me."

He hummed softly, gently squeezing my hand; his eyes reflected a glimmer of remorse.

"Think of it as penance." He said with a breathy sigh. "There's only one reason Phoenix would have brought you here. You have questions you need answers to. You want to know why you and your stay sister share a mirrored mark."

My heart bead rapidly in my chest as he spoke, and I fought not to wrench my hand from his.

Phoenix could sense apprehension, and he stood from his sent on the couch.

"Xy—"

"How the hell do you know about that?" I asked, trying my best not to seem defensive; that I was speaking through clenched teeth certainly wasn't helping. "How could you know anything about me or Areena, old man?"

His lips now held a somber smile, and he gently pulled me over to a weathered armchair.

"Come and sit." He said in a tone of melancholy. "It is time you knew who you are, who your parents are."

My heart was beating with equal parts eagerness and trepidation at Mr. Graeves' words. The implication of what he knew brought back desperate questions that I'd long since pushed down. I sat in the chair as I stared at the old man, Phoenix sitting at the end of the couch next to me—he wanted to be close in case I got stuck in my head again, if I had to guess—and beside him were Kaylen and Gerimy.

"I think I understand why you know some things you know." Kaylen hummed as he sat back in his seat. "You're an Empath. A rare trait among humans."

Mr. Graeves nodded with a hum.

"Aye." He said. "It's a trait passed down from generation to generation on my mother's side of the family."

He turned to look at Phoenix.

"It's how I knew you were an Alpha when we first met."

Phoenix's eyes widened as his head snapped towards his old mentor.

"You knew?"

"I may be an old man, Phoenix, but my senses as an Empath have not dulled."

I looked at him.

"But what does that have to do with anything?"

Mr. Graeves looked at me and chuckled, and it confused me a little.

Why was he laughing?

Was he making fun of me?

"What—?"

"It's the trait of some Empaths to be guarded against things they perceive to be threats." He said. "It appears you've inherited that trait from me."

My tongue swelled in my throat, and I felt my chest tighten.

My heartbeat rang in my ears as my mind replayed his words repeatedly like a track on repeat.

'What the hell is this old man?! Is he fucked in the head?!'

My thoughts pounded in my head.

"Xyla."

All at once, the warm touch of the wolf-shifter beside me silenced the noise and chaos from my spiraling thoughts. I looked at Phoenix, and while he looked to be just as shocked by the revelation as I was there, tending me in deep breaths.

"I apologize." Mr Graeves spoke, ruining the tender moment. "I know it must be a shock—"

"Well, that's a *fucking* understatement." I said as I looked at him. "How the hell else am I supposed to process that?!"

I gritted my teeth to keep myself from completely going off on the old man, and while I did my best to keep my composure and ignore the shocked wolf-shifters that were my company, Mr. Graeves just looked at me with eyes of remorse. It looked as though as he had known that this was the reaction that I would give, and I don't know why, but it pissed me off more.

"Well, I guess I deserve that." He said with a sigh. "Your mother tried so hard to keep this from happening. She's still trying, my poor darling. She blames herself for all of this."

I'd been about to say something when Phoenix gently squeezed my hand, stopping me from saying something I might regret.

"Mr. Graeves," he spoke calmly, "you mentioned Seraphim before, and you knew Xyla had been the one to tell me without even being told. How did you know? What exactly *is* Seraphim?"

The old man looked at Phoenix, then at me, and then he hummed.

"Yes, I suppose I should really start at the beginning." He said.

At his pause, I found myself leaning in despite the anxiety that was coursing through my veins. The old man seemed to collect his thoughts, and after he seemed to have done so, he spoke again.

"Seraphim refers to a particular vision, a prophecy foretold by the Oracle of Cathedral." He explained, though his words only gave rise to more questions. "Several years ago—twenty-seven, to be precise—the Oracle was found prostrate in her chamber, mumbling in a fit. She'd had visions before, but none had been so vivid that they drove her from her bed. It was that vision that foretold the battle that would shake the foundations of the city and herald a new era from the ruins of the old."

Mr. Graeves then turned his eye to me.

"Her vision spoke of mirror images fighting each other."

"Mirror images?" Gerimy asked.

"He means identical twins, or even rarer, mirror twins." Kaylen said. "With the latter, one twin is born with their organs mirrored on the opposite side from the other."

My hand shot to my right shoulder, where the mark of that blasted wing was.

Areena's wing was on her left shoulder, and mine was on my right.

"So, what exactly does that mean?" Gerimy asked, still confused.

Phoenix's hand gently squeezed mine, and I let out a shaky breath as I spoke.

"Seraphim comes from words that mean 'angel.'" I said. "Beings associated with light and purity... like an *Aster-Blood*."

"Yes. The Oracle's vision foretold the inevitable return of the *Aster-Bloods*, their 'next generation'." Mr. Graeves said. "And it was this interpretation that Director Caldwell became obsessed with."

My eyes widened, and I looked at the old man.

"How do you know that?" I asked. "There's no way that this could be known infor-mation within all of Cathedral. Phoenix said that you work in the Archives Division."

"I... have to agree..." Phoenix spoke, equally uneasy about the situation. "This wasn't in the file you gave me, either."

"And it wasn't in any information I gathered during my investigation." I said. "So, how do you know?"

The twitch of Mr. Graeves' hands was too subtle to escape my eye, and the surrounding air declined into a low temperature of despair and regret.

"When the Oracle received her vision, it was my unit that was there to ensure her safety. We'd been called because she'd sounded an alarm." Mr. Graeves said. "Director Caldwell was there, too, of course."

I raised an eyebrow at him.

"Your unit?"

"Yes, I was once a black ops agent." He answered. "I'd been assigned as one of her personal guard."

"This Oracle woman sounds rather important to Cathedral." Kaylen hummed, lean-ing his arms on his legs. "Who is she?"

Another twitch from the old man.

He took a deep breath and answered.

"She... is the last Morgenstern." He said, and he looked at me. "And it's the blood of Morgenstern that's mixed with vampire blood that gives Mesmers their ability."

"Any record of my bloodline would have burned up in the orphanage fire." I said. "It's impossible for anyone to know of those records even before then because they were sealed."

"And yet," he said, "it is a verifiable fact that anyone who was born a Mesmer has been a descendant of the Morgenstern bloodline."

"Yeah, but that means nothing when Claustus Morgenstern was a horn-dog who had multiple partners before he married Elaine." I said. "Her first-born was even a descendant of the Morgenstern line, a child of one of Claustus' several affairs."

"A Mesmer's ability comes from the union of vampire blood and a *direct* descendant of Morgenstern." Mr. Graeves said. "There are many who have the blood of Morgenstern in the city, but none of them have the ability as a Mesmer."

"This is making my head hurt." Gerimy muttered. "What is any of this supposed to mean? And what does it have to do with why we're here?"

I bit my lip; I knew what the implication was. Eshrik, the son of the Butterfly Killer, was born of the Morgenstern bloodline and the first generation blood of Elaine.

That fact made sense and proved that Mesmer abilities resulted from being a direct descendant of the Morgenstern bloodline.

And it certainly made sense that Areena and I were direct descendants of Lucien Morgenstern considering our ability

But Mr. Graeves' explanation raised a question.

"Can... the abilities of a Mesmer be passed down... like other traits?" I asked.

He looked at me again; he knew why I'd asked.

"Yes..." he said. "But that isn't the case with you and your sister. Your ability manifested much earlier than it had in your grandfather, your mother's father."

I was relieved, but it still raised the question about my mother.

And judging from what he'd said, I had a guess at what he was getting at.

But that wasn't the reason we were there.

"Why is Director Caldwell so obsessed with Seraphim?" I asked, getting back on topic; I needed to know why.

Phoenix's hand squeezed mine as he cleared his throat a little. Mr. Graeves let out a sigh as he sat back in his chair.

"I'm not sure." He said. "After we witnessed the Oracle's prophecy, he swore my unit and me to secrecy... and he became obsessed with it, the meaning of the words she spoke. He assigned another unit to watch over her..."

He squeezed his hands together as he took a breath.

"He... He—"

"He authorized the experiments on twins." Phoenix said. "He signed off on all of it."

"Experiments?" Kaylen's tone of disgust was clear as he spoke.

"Yes..." Mr Graeves confirmed. "My unit... we brought those children to him... it was an order that we didn't have the luxury of refusing, considering the oath he made us swear."

The remorse I'd seen now made sense; the blood of those children stained his hands.

"Mr. Graeves..." Phoenix muttered beside me.

The old man's eyes glistened with tears building, and he put a hand to his head, covering his eyes.

"Director Caldwell demanded that we bring him sets of twins born around the time of the Oracle's prophecy." He said, his voice cracking with regret. "We staggered the pairs...

not wanting to bring attention to any of the Investigators in the organization. And… when Caldwell was done with them, he tasked me with… disposing of the bodies…"

The words made an unnerving chill run down my spine; I could only imagine how sick he was feeling, having to talk about his part.

"I don't understand." Gerimy said. "What do twins have to do with your Oracle's prophecy?"

I wanted to smack the kid over the head, and I could tell that Kaylen wanted to yank on his brother's ear to keep him in line. Mr. Graeves answered the youngest brother's question.

"Director Caldwell didn't know how the 'mirror images' would be marked." He said, wiping his eyes. "He only deduced that the Oracle's prophecy spoke of twins. He was manic about it. He refused to listen to reason when it came to the unethical means of acquiring those children. He even spoke of murdering the parents just so that no one would go looking for them. After seeing those children mutilated at the end… I couldn't stand it anymore."

"You spoke out against him." Phoenix realized. "That's how you ended up in the Archives Division."

Mr. Graeves shifted in his seat, and he nodded.

"Yes." He said. "I spoke out. I'd had enough of taking those dead children, all cut up and bloody, to the furnaces beneath Cathedral… their small corpses burned."

"It was until the orphanage fire that those experiments stopped." Phoenix said. "And that could only mean one thing."

"Caldwell had found his Seraphim twins. Areena and myself." I muttered in disgust as I fought a shudder in my spine. "So, he set the fire to the orphanage?"

"It's a valid hypothesis." Phoenix said. "But it does seem—"

"Yes." Mr. Graeves said. "We didn't think he would find you… we didn't know how he could have known about you two being there. We'd hoped that the two of you would be safe in the system… your records sealed away…"

My head snapped to the old man, and I felt anger boil in my chest.

"'Safe…'" I muttered, my fingers clenching into my palms. "You both thought that we would be safe?!"

"Xyla—"

I wrenched my hand from Phoenix's, preventing him from calming me down as I stood up. My rage fueled the adrenaline that coursed through my veins in a fury, and I was close to pacing.

"Do you not know anything about the foster care system?" I glared at the man, clenching my hands into fists to keep them from shaking. "Do you have any idea what it was like for us?! We were alone! We were cast aside because of our eyes! No one even gave us a chance!"

Hot tears pooled in my eyes as let the years of pain I'd felt resurface and spew forth; I had pushed all of it down when I was younger, refusing to let them get the better of me.

But now, faced with one of the people who had put us in that place, I couldn't keep it down.

Phoenix stood up, slowly taking a step towards me. He reached out to touch me.

"Xy—"

"Who is she?" I asked, stepping forward to the old man. "Who is my mother? I want you to say it."

Mr. Graeves didn't look at me; it was as if he couldn't, like he was afraid of what he'd see.

"Look at me and say it!" I said, my tears streaming down my cheeks. "It's my right!"

"Xyla!"

I looked at Phoenix. His eyes were narrowed, glowing gold, and his teeth were nearly protruding from his lips.

It was the first time I'd seen him angry since I'd called him "lap dog" too many times when he'd helped me escape from the detention labyrinth.

I was half shocked and half enraged at his audacity; he knew what I'd gone through, the answers I wanted so desperately. I curled my fingers into my palms, gritting my teeth just as Phoenix took a deep breath to calm himself.

"Xyla, that's enough." He said, trying to defuse the situation.

"You have *no* right to tell me when it's enough." I said, jabbing my finger into his chest. "I've been wanting answers since I was a child! I have every right to them!"

"I understand—"

"*No*, you don't understand, Phoenix!" I said, tears coming from a different emotion altogether. "You understand nothing about me!"

There was so much more I wanted to say in that moment, but if I'd said anything else, I would have hurt Phoenix. I didn't know why I cared, but my conscience wouldn't let me lose my composure.

Phoenix reached his hand out to touch my cheek, and as much as I wanted that comforting touch, I pulled back from him. He looked hurt, and it only made me feel worse.

"Xy—"

"Don't." I said, wiping my eyes; I regained my composure with a deep breath and turned to leave the apartment.

"W-Wait, Xyla!" Phoenix called out.

"I want to be alone." I said.

I stopped as I put my hand on the doorknob. I closed my eyes, wondering if I should say anything. My mind was fighting itself about what I should do, and in the end, I opted to just leaving the apartment.

I needed time to breathe, to recollect my thoughts... and to stop myself from bursting into tears again.

8

A Secret to be Kept

Phoenix

"W-Wait, Xyla—"

"Let her go." Mr. Graeves said, putting his hand on my arm and shaking his head. "The girl has a lot to think about. I know that this has been a lot for her to take in."

He had a point; Xyla had just found out that her parents gave her and Areena up for adoption in order to keep them safe from Director Caldwell, that her parents were still alive.

Hell, it surprised me that Mr. Graeves was her father.

"Still..." I hummed, looking at the door. "I know she was angry... but—"

"She's justified in her anger." The old man sighed. "I know that she'd experienced heartache and horror in her life, and her path going forward will be just as treacherous, I'm afraid."

"What exactly was the prophecy your Oracle foretold?" Kaylen asked, sitting back against the sofa. "If you don't ask me asking, sir."

Mr. Graeves gave him a sad smile and let out a sigh before he looked at me. He gestured for me to sit in the armchair Xyla had been sitting in.

"'When the Tear of Cassius eclipses the full moon of the solstice, mirrors of one another will fight for the other's single wing, consuming their other half.'" The way he spoke told me he didn't have to think long about it. "'A new age will rise from the ruins of the old. So shall come the Seraphim.'"

The words were cryptic, and they certainly felt familiar; it reminded me of the woman in the cloak that had faced me from my cell in the detention labyrinth.

A realization hit me like a gut punch.

The woman had Xyla's face.

"The Oracle..." I swallowed a dry lump in my throat. "She's their mother... isn't she?"

Mr. Graeves took a deep breath—a thing I noticed he'd been doing a lot—and he nodded.

"Yes." He said. "The Oracle of Cathedral, the last Morgenstern, is Xyla's and Areena's mother... and I suspect that's why Director Caldwell had been adamant about finding Xyla. He wants to control the Herald of Seraphim."

My brow furrowed.

"Wait... 'the Herald?'" I asked. "I thought Seraphim referred to Xyla and Areena."

"No." He said. "I've... been in contact with the Oracle since she escaped her chamber room in Cathedral. The vision hasn't changed, but she's understood a deeper meaning of what she's seen. She's done a lot of research and meditation on her vision, looking for deeper meaning. She still means to prevent it, to spare Xyla and Areena in any way possible."

"And what's her new understanding?"

Mr. Graeves had been about to answer when he started coughing, and rather violently at that.

"S-She—"

The man couldn't catch his breath to say anything, and I stood from my seat.

"Mr. Graeves!" I said, kneeling beside him as he fought to breathe. "What's happening? What do you need?"

He coughed into a clenched fist and pointed to the kitchen.

"Me-Medicine..." He wheezed. "C-Cabinet..."

"I'll get it for you." Kaylen said as he went to the kitchen to retrieve it.

"And some water." I said, and I turned to look at Gerimy. "Find Xyla. Tell her—"

"N-No!" Mr. Graves wheezed as he grabbed my arm. "D-Don't... tell her..."

His blue-gray eyes were desperate, and my brow furrowed with confusion and hesitation. I respected the old man as a friend and mentor, but he was also Xyla's biological father; she needed to know that he was ill.

Though I understood why he wanted to keep it from her; it looked like it was a serious condition.

Kaylen came back with a medicine bottle and a glass of water. Mr. Graeves took the bottle with shaking hands, and as he struggled to open it, I gently took it from him and opened it.

"How many?" I asked.

Mr. Graeves coughed violently and held up two fingers. I got two pills out of the bottle for him, and he swallowed them along with a drink of water. I looked back at the bottle and my brow furrowed.

It was a prescription for a violent dry cough, but I had doubts that his condition was anything but severe. I'd hidden my surprise before when I saw him for the first time in a month; he was a lot thinner than he had been, and the tremor in his hands had gotten worse.

"Mr. Graeves?" I asked, gently putting my hand on his back as his coughing fit died down. "Are you—?"

"Sorry, lads." He said, his voice gravelly from his raw throat. "I need to rest for a while. Don't tell Xyla about this... please?"

I shared a look with Kaylen, who gave me a shrug; he looked just as unsure about his request as I was. I looked at Gerimy. His brother shot him a look as well. The young brother looked between me and his brother, and then he gave a sigh.

"Fuck, peer pressure." He grumbled. "Fine."

I looked at Mr. Graeves as he stood, and I helped him to his room. I looked at the brothers.

"Secure the floor." I said. "And check on Xyla. Make sure she's alright."

The two of them nodded and then left the apartment. The old man gave a tired chuckle.

"I thought so." He said as he looked at me with a smile. "You're definitely an Alpha."

I flinched at his words without meaning to. I shouldn't have been surprised that he knew; with what Kaylen said about him being an Empath, it made sense.

"I'm not an Alpha." I said as I helped him into bed. "I... ran away from it all instead of facing it... if anything, I'm a coward—"

"Nonsense." He said, gently taking my hand. "You, Phoenix Bryte, are not a coward. You've always one to question everything. You have such strong moral fiber."

"But..." I said, "it was because of that moral fiber that I left my Pack..."

Guilt simmered in my gut at the thought of Sareena, how I'd practically led her to death just because I trusted her enough to be my partner in leading the Pack.

'No.' I thought as I fought to not grit my teeth. 'It was Joshuah who killed her... the bastard...'

"Phoenix." Mr. Graeves said as he squeezed my hand. "Don't blame yourself for what happened. Let go of that guilt before it completely ruins you."

It was hard not to feel a little... *violated*... whenever the old man read my emotions like that, but I understood why he said what he did; he was only trying to help. It was the kind of person he was, with or without his ability as an Empath.

"And don't forget," he said, smiling, "you have Xyla with you. You both need each other, whether or not she realizes it."

My heart sank a little.

"I'm not sure—"

"Give her time." He chuckled softly, fighting off a bit of a cough. "She's... definitely got her ancestor's—*my* ancestor's—fighting spirit, and her mother's caring heart..."

My brow furrowed at his words; I knew that her mother was the last Morgenstern, but who was Xyla's ancestor?

"Her ancestor..." I hummed a little. "Mr. Graeves, who—?"

The old man's chest rose and fell gently, and when I looked at his face, I didn't say another word.

He was asleep, and given his condition, he needed his rest. I let out a sigh and stood from his bedside. I slowly closed the door to his room, and I walked back to the living room. I still had so many questions for Mr. Graeves, but I decided to keep them for later. I sat back in the armchair and rubbed my eyes with a sigh.

Things were getting a lot more complicated than they were supposed to be.

9

How He Sees Xyla Coltt

Kaylen

I WILLED MY IRRITATION away, trying not to think about how Gerimy outright refused to find the woman, Xyla Coltt. I was beginning to think he wasn't taking this mission seriously. Had it not been for Lexy's insistence on bringing him with me to follow Phoenix, I would have left him behind at the Den.

I shook my head slightly.

'Gerimy is still a child... or at least, that's how he acts...'

In all honesty, had I left my foolish younger brother behind, he would have only been used as a tool to torture Lexy, or worse, he would have been tortured himself. The three of us were the only family we had left; I couldn't abandon that bond so haphazardly.

I pushed the matter out of my mind and followed Xyla's scent; she smelled like vanilla and cinnamon, but it wasn't overpowering.

It was easy to follow.

I followed the scent to the fire escape, where I found the woman sitting on the metal stairs. Her white hair was flowing behind her in the nighttime breeze, and her eyes were narrowed, focusing on her hands as they clenched into fists and relaxed.

I recognized the method; it was a form of stress relief that I'd seen my Celia use whenever she felt overwhelmed.

But from the way the woman's jaw was set, I could tell that it wasn't working for her; the conversation with the old man had apparently rattled her.

'She was an orphan for the longest time.' I reminded myself. 'Her reaction to all of this is justified... though she does have a tendency to let her temper get the better of her, I've noticed.'

"Did Phoenix tell you to come and find me?"

I jumped a little when she addressed me. She hadn't looked up when I'd opened the door, and I thought she'd simply been ignoring me.

"No." I answered truthfully. "He only said to make sure you were alright."

She hummed a little as she reclined on the rusty stairwell, stretching her legs out and resting on her elbows on the step behind her.

"Yeah, that sounds like him..." She sighed.

The tone she spoke with made my brow furrow, and I tilted my head a little.

"Are you... displeased?" I asked; when she looked at me with a raised eyebrow, I elaborated. "With Phoenix, I mean."

"What? No, of course not." She said, answering quicker than I thought she would. "Why would you think that?"

She seemed shocked that I'd asked her such a question.

"Then... why the melancholy?"

She narrowed her eyes a little and then sighed, relaxing once again as she looked out at the city. She seemed to contemplate the answer, as if she didn't know why herself. Figuring she wasn't about to answer, I turned to head back inside to the apartment.

"All this time," she suddenly spoke, shocking me, "I had wished that the reason my sister and I were at that orphanage was that our parents were dead."

I turned back to look at her as she sat up and ran a hand through her hair with a sigh.

"I guess... I'm more upset that everything Mr. Graeves had told us makes sense... even if it goes against what I believed until now." She let out a dry chuckle at the end. "I'm not sure what I believe anymore."

I raised an eyebrow at her.

"What you believe?"

She stood from the stairs as she kept her eyes on the light of the city. She stretched her arms behind her with a hum.

"Never in my life have I ever considered fate or destiny to be legitimate." She said. "I've always hated the idea that people aren't in control of their own lives, that every choice made is not one of our own free will."

I stared at her, watching her strong posture and how she held herself.

Xyla Coltt was nothing like I'd imagined her to be when I'd heard that she was the leader of the Black Wing Group. I'd imagined her as a savage militant like Brine Coltt was, a brute who only wanted battle and chaos as if it were necessary for survival. But as she spoke, I saw her in a different light; the way she stood and the way she spoke told me she had a compassionate heart and a level head on her shoulders. She wouldn't make a move unless she thought through every step of the process and the consequences of her actions. She was careful, a trait of a strong leader.

A leader worthy of the title of Luna if she accepted the Bond between her and Phoenix.

She let out a sigh and turned to me.

"You asked if I was displeased with Phoenix." She said. "My answer is still no. I'm not 'displeased' with him… it's just… I'm not sure if I completely buy into the whole *animae nexum* thing."

I guess I shouldn't have been surprised, considering how she thought.

"But why… if I may ask?"

"I guess the entire philosophy of it and hatred of the idea of destiny." She shrugged with a dry chuckle. "Besides, after all I've lost, I don't think I could handle opening up to anyone like that."

Her eye twitched, and her brow furrowed. She rubbed her temple and let out a sigh. She looked at me.

"Just… forget I said anything…" She said, waving off her words. "Let's get back to the apartment before Phoenix freaks out."

Her words puzzled me; I really hadn't known the Alpha to freak out, and I'd known him since we were all children. Before I could comment on it, she started walking towards men and the door.

And then, for the first time since I'd met her, a small smile appeared on her lips.

"Come on, Kaylen." She said. "I think I've cooled off enough now."

She had an air about her that was like Phoenix's, and I found myself following her just as I would him. I closed the door behind us and walked down the hallway to the apartment with her.

Our Luna, Xyla Coltt.

10

THE PLAN MOVING FORWARD

Phoenix

I RUBBED MY TEMPLES as I tried to make sense of the info dump I'd been given—that *we'd* been given—by Mr. Graeves. The silence of the apartment afforded me the headspace for me to really think through what we'd been told. It was all too surreal, and thinking about it only made my head pound like a drum.

"Alpha."

I looked up to see Gerimy; he was holding a water bottle out towards me; it was one of the many that Xyla had packed for the trek across the city to Mr. Graeves' apartment.

"Here." He said. "You look like you need it."

I nodded and took the bottle from him.

"Thanks." I said as I twisted the cap off the bottle. "What's your report?"

"The building is secure." He said. "There aren't that many residents on this floor, so it was a clean sweep."

"And Xyla?" I asked.

"Kaylen followed her scent. My guess was that she went to the fire escape." He paused, and then he spoke again. "Alpha, can I ask you something?"

I looked at him with a raised eyebrow as I set the bottle down on the table.

"Asking if you can ask me something is already asking me something." I said. "Just ask what you want to ask."

I had a feeling of what he was going to ask; it was better to get it out of the way.

Gerimy seemed to hesitate as he gnawed on the inside of his cheek, and then, with a sharp inhale, he looked at me.

"Why that woman?" He asked. "Why make so much effort for that woman's affection when she clearly doesn't accept the Bond?"

And there it was.

I had to remind myself that out of the three Crescent siblings, Gerimy was the youngest and hadn't found his *animae nexum*. Even explaining why I did what I did for Xyla would be hard, because he didn't understand the gravity of such a connection. The strongest connection for him was to his siblings, and both of them had found their mates.

Either way, he was expecting an answer, and as one of the youngest shifters in the Pack. He needed to have something to build off, at least.

"I put in the effort because she needs someone." I said. "She's been fighting this battle all on her own, and it's taken its toll on her. I can understand a bit of what she's going through."

The young shifter's eyes furrowed, and he sighed.

"That woman is baffling." He said as he crossed his arms, leaning against the kitchen counter as he spoke freely. "She knows that her twin sister isn't a good person; she's the very enemy she's been investigating all this time. Yet, she clings to hope that she can reach her."

His words revealed he was more than a little peeved, and I couldn't blame him for that. I was just as aggravated, but it was more with myself than with Xyla's denial; I knew better than anyone that she was hurting, and that what we'd learned that night had affected her more than the rest of us.

I knew all that, and I still reacted so harshly towards her when she learned the truth, that Mr. Graeves was her father and that her mother was the last Morgenstern princess.

"Leave Xyla alone for now."

I turned my head to see Mr. Graeves standing in the hall that led to the bedrooms. He wiped a handkerchief over his forehead and straightened his glasses; he looked a little better than he had before, but I knew looks could be deceiving.

"Should you really be up and about, old man?" Gerimy asked. "One wrong move and you could keel over. Xyla would know that you're ill."

"Gerimy!" I hissed, snapping my head towards him. "Mind your manners!"

"It's fine, both of you." He said. "There is much that you lot need to prepare for, and Xyla, especially, given what path lies ahead of her."

I recalled the Oracle's prophecy. Just thinking about it set my teeth on edge.

"You can't seriously expect her to fight against Areena." I said, as if I were the one trying to reason with Fate itself instead of Xyla. "Not after all she's gone through. She's spent the better part of a month trying to find her after realizing she was still alive."

Mr. Graeves heaved a sigh, and he took off his glasses. He rubbed his eyes a little before placing his glasses on his nose again.

"Unfortunately, she'll have to." He said. "With how that man has corrupted and manipulated Areena, getting through to her will be difficult, and the way things are about to unfold will only test her will all the more."

His words were cryptic, and the grit in my teeth grew worse.

"We can't stay here forever." I said. "Cathedral is still be looking for us, and now that we've confirmed that they, the Rising, and Joshuah are all involved, they'll locate us before long."

"Not necessarily." Mr. Graeves said. "Cathedral will be more focused on security for the festivities next summer. It's already promising to be quite the event of the era."

My brows knit together at the old man's words; had summer really passed us by during our stay at the Den and the recuperation at Xyla's old hideout?

"What festivities?" Gerimy asked. "Why would Cathedral care about some festival?"

"It's not *just* a festival."

I turned my head to see Xyla and Kaylen; the latter had been the one who'd spoken. Kaylen sighed as he walked in.

"Geez, you didn't pay attention in school, did you?"

"What's that supposed to mean?" Gerimy gritted his teeth, crossing his arms childishly. "What's so important about it?"

"The event in question is the Summer Soiree." I said, realizing the event Mr. Graeves was talking about. "Cathedral always does security for it, and they'll be wanting to prepare for any disturbance."

Gerimy raised an eyebrow.

"What's a sweary?"

"Soiree!" The four of us corrected his blatant butchering.

"The Summer Soiree takes place during the Solstice," Xyla explained, leaning against the armrest of the chair in the living room; "and it's a festival to showcase the businesses of Arboriah City. It's an age old tradition."

"It's also a holiday that celebrates the heroism of Arboriah Lux and Esilas Solani." Mr. Graeves added. "And next year, there is an astronomical event. The return of Cassius' Comet and a full moon."

The information was perplexing, and I didn't understand the significance of it. A look around the room told me that the others didn't know what it meant, either. My former mentor hummed softly, seeing our confusion, and he explained the meaning of it all.

"The prophecy that the Oracle witnessed around the time of your conception foretold of an event that would take place around the return of Cassius' Comet." Mr. Graeves said as he turned to look at the only woman in the room. "The prophecy of Seraphim."

I looked at Xyla, worried that she would get upset again; however, she remained calm, taking a deep breath before she nodded.

"So... we have an idea about the timeframe of their plans." She said. "Whatever Vanguard Hollum is planning, it'll happen next year during the solstice."

"There's also the slight problem of Joshuah and his hold over the Pack." Kaylen said. "We don't know what the Rising has planned for them and the Black Wing Group."

That issue was definitely one of the more troublesome ones; we didn't know what Joshuah had done with those who rebelled against him and his coalition with the Group and the Rising.

In truth, we didn't know who was on our side in that conflict at all.

Realization of how rock the road ahead of us was fell over the apartment in a stiff silence, and as time went on, it grew more and more palpable, nearly thick enough to smother. My eyes were on Xyla, and her eyes reflected the battle she had with herself. She always seemed to fight with herself, and I could imagine what the conflict was at the moment.

"You four should get some rest." Mr. Graeves said, clearing his throat as he broke the silence while making the atmosphere more awkward at the same time. "Decisions shouldn't be made with weary minds. Discuss the subject in the morning."

I couldn't stop myself from cracking a smile; Mr. Graeves was always the kind to look out for someone.

He had when he took me in, after all.

"I agree." Xyla said, looking at me and the brothers. "I think we've had enough excitement for today."

The three of us agree, and Mr. Graeves walked over to us.

"Xyla can have the guest room." He said. "I wish I had the room to accommodate the rest of you comfortably, but you'll have to share the living room."

Gerimy grumbled beside me and then flinched with a groan as Kaylen smacked him across the back of the head.

"We appreciate it, Mr. Graeves. Thank you." I bowed my head, respectively.

He smiled and nodded to me in return. He left the room and returned moments later with blankets and pillows. I had to bite back a smile, remembering how Xyla's hospitality at the tavern apartment had been similar.

Mr. Graeves escorted his daughter to the guest room, and I looked around the room once again. I had so many memories in that place; it was surprising how things always came full circle.

The Den to the City.

The City to the Outskirts.

11

HER HATRED FOR HER SISTER

Areena

I SPIT OFF TO the side as I stood to my feet to face my opponent once more. I narrowed my eyes at the rabid mongrel—one of the shifter prisoners used as "training dummies" with a bit of suggestion from my vanguard—who snarled at me.

"Stop reacting and fight!"

Hollum's "words of wisdom" were more distraction to me than they were helpful; he'd been on my case about training since I'd purposely missed the last lesson.

The shifter howled and lunged at me with foaming teeth. I clenched my jaw and lunged as well, a knife in my hand.

"Don't even think about using your Mesmer ability!" He shouted.

It had only crossed my mind for a moment, and somehow he knew.

He *always* knew.

I gritted my teeth, roaring in frustration as I swung my knife at the rabid shifter.

Smack!

The knife flew from my grasp as my opponent pummeled me to the ground, pinned in place by massive paws. Rancid breath crawled along my skin as the gnarled muzzle bared teeth at me in a vicious growl.

I dared to look in the beast's eyes, narrowing my own at this mongrel's audacity.

I was angry.

Angry that I'd let my frustration get the better of me in a fight, even if it was just a training battle.

Angry at Hollum and his cryptic words as he forced me into these lessons.

Angry that I was in this situation at all.

All because my *beloved* sister broke her promise to me.

I gritted my teeth and reached my hands up to grab the mongrel by the throat, an action that shocked him from his rampage. My fingers plunged into his fur, grabbing his throat.

I pushed the beast back, getting to my feet as my fingers dug into flesh.

My right side felt heavier, my wing having manifested from the mark on the back, and the beast's eyes reflected horror.

My eyes narrowed.

I didn't want to be choking the life out of one of Hollum's mindless beasts; I wanted to be strangling Xyla, to make her look at me in the eyes and see the monster she'd made.

The beast writhed in my grasp, the blood vessels in its eyes pulsing and bursting in his panic.

Snap!

The beast fell limp from my hold and on to the training room's floor. It lay there still, its chest not even moving with breath.

I pulled back and looked at my hands, the tips of my fingers—more specifically, my nails that had sharpened into long claws—painted in sticky red.

Blood.

Clap.

Clap.

Clap.

My head snapped towards my vanguard; he was slowly clapping, an evilly satisfied grin on his face. The look alone sent chills rippling down my spine and prickling along my skin.

"Well done, my dove!" He said, his voice dripping with ecstatic joy. "You're now ready for the next stage!"

The way he said it made the hair on the back of my neck stand on end, and every muscle in my body tensed, as if waiting for a strike.

Vanguard Hollum had changed since Xyla's capture and subsequent escape.

He'd been obsessed with Seraphim, how the two of us were destined to fight and one of us killing the other.

His obsession had turned manic now.

He gestured at me with two fingers, beckoning me like a child or some passive animal.

As much as I hated the reflex, I walked over to him. He put his fingers on my chin and made me focus on his eyes.

"It's time for the next step."

Before I could even form a thought, my mind sank into a sea of pinkish gold, and my body felt light as a feather.

12

ACCEPTANCE

Xyla

I TOSSED AND TURNED in bed, my mind swimming with thoughts. My pulse raced with the speed of such intrusive inklings, and the mark on my shoulder thrummed with pain. My fingers curled into the sheets, and I could feel my nails ripping through the fabric.

A spike of adrenaline shot through my veins, and I shot upright in bed, a cold sweat sticking to my skin. My wing had manifested, a dull ache in my shoulder at the weight. I let out a breath and closed my eyes as I ran my fingers through my hair, and I felt something odd. I looked at my hands, and my heartbeat quickened.

My nails were long and sharp, almost like claws.

They were bloody; I'd scratched my head when I was running my fingers through my hair.

I took deep breaths, trying to calm my rising anxiety. Gradually, the nails sank back like cat claws, and after that had been dealt with, I focused on merging my wing back into my shoulder. I let out a sigh of relief, and I buried my face in my hands.

'What the hell is happening to me?'

Luka's voice didn't answer; he hadn't spoken since first getting to Mr. Graeves' apartment.

'What a convenient time for him not to respond...'

I still didn't know if it was just imagination or if it was his ghost, but it was still comforting in a way. It was a comfort I needed at that moment.

I tapped my fingers against the mattress with muffled thumps as I chewed my bottom lip in thought; there was no way I was getting any sleep after all that.

I rubbed my eyes with a sigh.

"The last thing I need is insomnia..."

I threw off the covers as I swung my legs over the side of the bed. My feet flattened against old matted carpet, and I carefully stood to leave the guest room, careful not to step on any creaky floorboards.

The sounds of soft snores of three wolf-shifters filled the living room as I left the privacy of the guest room; Gerimy was probably the loudest of them. I could only wonder how Kaylen and Phoenix could sleep through the noise. Kaylen was asleep on the floor, and Phoenix was still as a board on the couch.

Huh, they were sleeping more comfortably than I thought they would; I guessed they had a lot of practice from the time we spent at the old tavern.

I made light steps towards the front door, knowing full well that I couldn't clear my mind with Gerimy's snoring. But once I got to the door, I just stared at the doorknob.

I was... hesitating?

Since when did I *ever* hesitate?

That time when Phoenix helped me escape the detention cells at Cathedral didn't count as hesitation, surely; Luka's voice had been echoing in my head about not killing him, and I'd only knocked him unconscious out of frustration.

I gritted my teeth together, trying to steel my nerves and take action.

I just wanted to get some air, a quiet place to think... it wasn't like I was going to leave them behind.

And then the thought occurred to me; why was I still hanging around?

Why hadn't I left Phoenix and the others behind before then?

What good would it have done to keep going along with them?

They were only going to be used against me if I continued to care about any of them, about Phoenix.

I curled my fingers into my palms, hating the parts of me that were battling against each other.

'It's fine.' I reassured myself. 'It's not like I'm actually leaving... am I?'

"Xyla...?"

I flinched at the sleepy voice that called my name, and I spun on my heels to face the one who had spoken.

It was Phoenix, his chest bare save for the still-healing bruises and scars that adorned his torso. His dark hair was disheveled from sleep.

"Xy? What are you doing up?" He hummed, his voice gravelly from sleep, but that wasn't why my heart tightened in my chest.

He'd called me by that nickname again. I fought the heat that threatened to flush my cheeks with color.

"I'm... just going out for some air..." I said. "I need a place to think."

He looked at me and sighed before grabbing his shirt and standing up from the couch. I raised an eyebrow at him.

"What are you doing?" I asked.

"I'm going with you." He answered.

"I need the quiet."

"I can be quiet."

Phoenix's golden eyes held a challenging fire to them, and we both knew that standing there and arguing about whether or not he would accompany me would only wake the others.

I let out a sigh and nodded.

"Alright. Fine." I said.

Phoenix's lips pulled into a sleepy grin, and he opened the door, stepping aside for me to leave first. I could only shake my head at his manners.

He was so very odd.

The two of us left the apartment and went to the fire escape I'd gone to before. I sat on the stairs, looking at the glowing structures of glass and steel that faded into brick. The light pollution was atrocious, blinding the natural light of the few stars that had returned to the sky; I'd been able to see them when we were at the Den, and I found myself missing that sight.

"What's on your mind, Xy?" Phoenix asked, breaking the blissful silence between us. "Talk to me... don't shut me out."

I looked at him as he leaned against the rusted railing. The cool breeze of the night tousled his hair.

'Trying to do damage control...' I thought to myself.

"Xyla, talk to him. It can't do you any harm to let him know how you're feeling." Luka's voice spoke, almost in a scolding manner; it was like I was a child again.

It took everything in me not to let out a scoff.

"You can't keep your emotions locked away forever."

I looked back at the city, a sigh escaping my lips.

"It's all too much…" I said, after a moment of thought. "What a fucking mess this all is… All of this because some egomaniac wants a grab for power, and he's using the Oracle's premonition and my sister and me to justify it all. It makes me angry."

"I know. It's a puzzle, that's for sure." Phoenix said. "I don't understand what Cathedral and the Rising have to do with each other, though."

I blinked at him, my lips parting slightly; did he seriously not know?

Had he seriously not figured it out by now?

I mean, yeah, Trackers were the lowest tier agents in the organization, but surely he would have realized that something was up before he and I had met during that chase.

I bit my lip a little.

Would he even believe me if I told him the truth, the reason he and I met the way we did?

"Phoenix—"

"I know that something's been screwy with Cathedral for a while now… but I decided to remain blind to it."

So he did notice; he just kept his head down and didn't say anything. Honestly, it was a smart move… or at least, it would have been before our time in the interrogation room. I'd pushed him to start digging deeper; he was perhaps one of the few moral agents in Cathedral.

The shifter ran his fingers through his hair as he dropped his head. It was almost as if he blamed himself for what was happening.

"Had I been more mindful of everything back then, would things be different now?" He asked. "Would I even be here?"

Something stabbed at my heart as he spoke, his voice on the verge of breaking; he wasn't just talking about Cathedral's director and what he'd done.

No, he was thinking about his brother's betrayal and the death of his wife.

I stood from my place on the stairs and took a step towards him.

"Phoenix—"

"And then there's you." He said, making me stop from reaching my hand out to him.

"Wait, me?" I asked. "What do you mean?"

"Just… you…" He said as he pushed himself off the railing and turned to look at me. "You.. the enigma that you are…"

His gaze was intense, and I fought the feeling of intimidation that crept up my spine. His hand found its way to my cheek, his palm caressing me gently as the tips of his fingers curled into my hair. No matter how hard I tried to fight it, I couldn't stop the heat that flushed to my cheeks as he slowly leaned in. His lips parted a little as he looked at mine.

"I don't want to push this on you." He whispered, his eyes softening their gaze. "If you want me to stop... then say so."

His breath lingered on my lips; he was only a few inches away now. My heart leapt in my chest when I realized what he was hinting at; this was his way of asking permission, and he was apologizing for being so bold.

My heartbeat quickened its pace, and my skin grew warmer. I wanted him to close the gap, but I couldn't get the words to come out. My fingers curled into my palms, and I willed myself to move.

And to my surprise, my body actually listened this time.

I closed the gap myself, brushing my lips against his in an awkward fever of emotion.

Phoenix's form was rigid, and I'd worried that I'd embarrassed myself; however, before I could pull away, his hand cradled the back of my head and deepened the kiss.

I could feel his heartbeat in his touch; it pulsed in sync with my own in my ears as a sensation of bliss thrummed through my chest.

My eyes closed just as Phoenix pulled away. He rested his forehead against mine, his breathing fanning my lips as mine did the same to his.

"Does this mean..." he whispered, "that you've accepted me?"

His tone held a twinge of insecurity; he was afraid that he'd forced me to react.

I could feel that much from him.

I let out an exasperated sigh, and I wrapped my arms around his neck, draping my arms off his shoulders.

"Silly." I said, opening my eyes to look at him; he looked like a shy schoolboy confessing to his crush. "I should be the one asking if you accept me, not the other way around."

His other arm wrapped around my waist as his hand tangled itself in my hair. His muscles seemed to breathe with ease as his heat encircled me. I'm pretty sure that if he was in his wolf form, his tail would wag like an excited puppy.

"You have no idea how long I've felt so empty." He whispered, his voice shaking with tender relief. "I've never felt so... *complete.*"

He sounded like he was about to cry, and my throat tightened with that same emotion.

I realized then just how empty I'd felt for as long as I could remember, how relieved I felt now that I'd taken the leap with swallowed courage.

It was at that moment that I felt Luka smiling; he was proud.

"You're no longer afraid, Xy." His voice echoed softly. *"I am proud of you... it means that you're almost ready..."*

My heart skipped at those words, and there was a familiar fear tightening in my chest.

What did Luka mean by that?

I hugged Phoenix a little tighter.

And... why did he sound so... sad?

13

DISTRACTIONS AND WARNINGS

Jaye

I SAT ALONE AT Solani's, hidden away in a corner booth as I watched the patrons. There were small parties of coworkers, a happy couple or two, the struggling office worker—as cliche as it sounded. All of them were citizens going about their normal lives.

I couldn't count myself among them anymore, not with what Old Man Graeves had told me about that woman and her sister.

Twins destined to fight each other until one of them died, and the victor gained the second wing.

Herald of Seraphim.

It sounded like something from a fae tale.

But then again, the Gods' Tree at the Den had once been considered a religious myth, and it was real.

I thought back to the Den, the image of my *animae nexum* bringing my mind back there.

"Lex..." I muttered, running my fingers over my palm.

My mind returned to the worry that I'd been trying to distract myself from; it had been over a month since the skirmish at the Den, and I didn't know what happened after I'd left. I could still feel the thrum of the Bond between the two of us, which meant that she was alive, but what about the baby?

I hated I couldn't be there to support her, and I could only imagine what she was going through. I fought the urge to grit my fangs, thinking of how Joshuah Bryte might have been treating her.

'If he's touched a hair on her head, I'll kill him myself.'

My resolve was firm, and it was hard not to show an outward reaction.

After all, I was still being watched; there was an agent in street clothes sitting in the booth near the door.

I could feel his eyes on me, not like he was being discreet about it, anyway.

'They're trying to see if I'll contact Phoenix.' I deduced; it was a conclusion that was the only plausible one.

Bzzzzt...

Bzzzzt...

I looked at my phone as the screen illuminated with a notification. I picked up my phone, and my heart leapt in my chest at the words from the screen.

"Target Acquired. Last seen entering low-income housing building in the Outer District."

There was only one reason Phoenix would decide to go there; it was where Old Man Graeves lived.

I cursed myself in my brain; I should have known that the old man would be under surveillance, too.

I got up, noticing that my shadow was still looking at me, and I walked over to the bar. I needed to contact the old man and warn him, but I couldn't do it with my phone; I had no doubts it had been bugged. I sat at the bar, and the bartender with a tattoo on his neck of a shield with a morning star sigil walked over to me.

"Jaye, what ya need, bud?" He asked; his name was Drakken, a former service buddy of mine. "Ya doing okay?"

"Doing well, all things considering." I said with a sigh.

He raised an eyebrow at me as he wiped the glass in his hand.

"Just well?" He asked. "You still working in the organization? You're not a sniper still, are ya?"

Drakken knew better than most that I hated being a puppet in the black ops group; he'd been a spotter for me as well as a tank on the battlefield. He had more scars than I did, physically, but we were both matched for the damage we took during our service.

"I'm an Investigator." I said. "But... this case I'm on is tough..."

He set the glass to the side and looked at me with all seriousness in his eyes.

"You weren't involved with that business at the Den, were ya?" He asked in a low tone.

"I was..." I said, "but that's not even the bulk of my worries."

"Then what is?"

I looked at him and then tapped on the counter in a code. I typed two letters.

A.N.

Drakken's eyes widened, and he looked at me.

"Wait... ya found *animae nexum*?" He asked. "Didn't think ya believed in that."

"It's not something you necessarily believe in, Drak." I said. "It just... happened."

"So, yer worried about them?" He asked. "That's normal."

"Well... it goes a little deeper than that..." I said. "She's at the Den... and she's the one that incited the rebellion."

"Oh, fuck." He said, hanging his head a little. "She's not—"

"No, she's still alive." I said. "I can feel that much."

"Then what's the issue?"

All I had to do was I look at him, and his eyes widened.

"Holy fuck, you're not serious..."

"I am." I said. "And she is."

He smeared his hand down his face.

"What are you going to do?" He asked.

"Well, I can't really do anything right now."

His eyebrow twitched into an arch.

"Wait, what do you mean by that?"

I scratched the side of my neck and subtly gestured to the booth where my shadow was observing me. Drakken's eyes flicked to where I'd been gesturing, and he hummed.

"Ah, yer being tailed."

I nodded and looked at him. An idea wormed its way into my brain, and I leaned against the bar.

"Think you could give me a shot?" I asked.

There was a glint of mischief in his eye, and his lips spread into a grin. He set a glass and a bottle in front of me before walking to the back. I poured a shot and downed it. It was an attempt to steel my nerves. I looked at the bottle and then pushed it off the bar-top.

Crash.

The bottle shattered on the tile floor.

In the service, the phrase was often used to give a distraction. I wondered what Drakken would do.

Drakken came around the bar and took me up by the collar, baring his teeth in a growl as he got in my face.

"Ya piece a shit!" He barked as he slammed me against the bar, bashing my head once against the bar-top.

The commotion was enough to cause a scene.

"Ya think just cuz yer an Investigator at Cathedral that ya can skip out on yer bill?!" He shouted, snarling in fury. "Ya high and mighty bastards piss me off!"

He kept shaking me by the collar, "beating" me to get his point across. The patrons cheered him on as he delivered a *very* real right hook to my jaw and a jab to my abdomen. I felt bad for giving them a show like this, but it was enough of a ruckus to distract the agent that was tailing me.

Drakken grabbed me by the back of the neck like I was a rabid dog and started dragging me to the back door. He shoved me into the wall in the alleyway. As soon as he shut the door, he hit the button on an old radio that started... playing fight noises?

I looked at him as I leaned against the wall, holding my stomach.

"Here." Drakken said as he pulled a cold beer from a cooler beside the door and tossed it to me. "Didn't mean to hit ya that hard, but I had to make it look good for the audience."

I caught the cold can and put it to the sore spot on my jaw. I raised an eyebrow at him.

"How often do you do things like this?" I asked, gesturing to his setup. "Has to be more than once."

Drakken leaned against the door as he pulled a cigarette box and lighter from his apron pocket.

"Guess ya can say that it's a Solani's tradition." He said. "We were a mob club at one point. The ruse was one of the best ways to get important figures out."

"Starting a fight to cause a distraction that would preoccupy the ones they're trying to get away from." I nodded. "Well, when I said 'give me a shot,' I definitely wasn't expecting a beating."

"Ya needed a distraction, so I got ya one." Drakken said as he lit his cigarette.

I chuckled softly and then opened the beer.

"Well, you never could back down from a fight." I said, before taking a sip.

Drakken let out a stream of smoke and then let out a sigh.

"So," he said as he crossed his arms, "wanna tell me why Cathedral got ya tailed?"

I looked at him. I didn't really have much of a choice; he'd end up hearing about it from other Investigators should something happen.

"This stays between us." I said. "I have your word on that, don't I?"

"Anything for a fellow ex-soldier." He said, flicking the cigarette ash. "So, what ya do?"

I took a deep breath as I let my head rest against the wall. I brought him up to speed on the situation.

I told him about Xyla Coltt and Phoenix breaking her out.

I told him what I knew thanks to the surveillance I was doing at the Den.

I could only imagine what Drakken thought about the choices that were made.

"So, Cathedral is in bed with the Rising and the Black Wing Group, huh?" He scoffed. "That doesn't make a lick of sense."

"This runs deeper than either of us knows." I said. "I just can't see the connection. Not yet, anyway."

Drakken hummed softly and then took another drag from his cigarette.

"Maybe that woman knows more than she's letting on."

"Xyla, you mean."

"No, I mean the girl from the show house in the next district over." He said, his face carrying a blank expression and his voice dry with sarcasm. "No shit I mean Xyla."

"Is the sarcasm really necessary?" I asked.

"In this case, it is." He answered. "From what you told me, that woman might know more about this whole situation."

He did have a point; Xyla's motives for everything reached far deeper than just a desire to be reunited with her sister. She'd even told Phoenix something that drove him to dig deeper into the mystery himself.

"You have a point."

Drakken nodded to me and then crushed the head of his cigarette into the wall.

"Find her, and you might find your answers."

I remembered the situation, the danger that Old Man Graeves and Phoenix's group were in, and I looked at my buddy.

"I need your phone."

He didn't say a word, only digging into his pocket and pulling out his phone.

"If you're being tailed, your phone is definitely bugged." He said as he tossed it to me. "Call your friends."

I caught the phone and dialed the old man's apartment.

"Thanks for this, Drak."

He simply chuckled and held out his arm to me. I grabbed his arm, a gesture that we used during our time in black-ops.

"Ya saved my life more than once in the service, bud." He said. "I don't mind taking the heat for ya on this."

Drakken was probably the most stand-up man I'd ever known. I hated to leave him with the trouble, but I knew he wasn't going to let me refuse his help.

"Get going while yer tail is distracted." He said with that familiar mischievous grin. "He'll know that something is up if yer still here."

I'd been about to say something when he let go of my arm and pushed me away. He then reached for the door, turning off the old radio.

"On with ya, now!" He yelled. "Scram!"

I nodded and turned to run down the alleyway and head towards my car. I held the phone up to my ear as I got into my car and started driving towards the Outer District.

Brrrrrring...

Brrrrrring...

"Dammit, Graeves. Pick up the damn phone!"

Brrrrrring...

When the phone finally picked up, the voice on the other side didn't belong to Graeves.

"Uh... Graeves' residence?"

The voice was that of a younger male; my guess was that it was one of the other two wolf-shifters that left with Phoenix and Xyla when they escaped the Den.

"Tell Bryte that the four of you have been spotted." I said, ignoring my desire to ask for Phoenix, to talk with him and make sure that he was alright. "You guys need to get out of that building now. They're coming."

14

ESCAPE INTO THE NIGHT

Phoenix

I HEARD THE REVVING engines before they appeared. I looked down the street just as the engines hushed and the headlights went out. It might have been dark, but I caught the movement of figures forming up.

Battle formations.

"Fuck, we've been made." I said, making Xyla crouch alongside me.

"How could Cathedral have known we're here?" She asked. "Would the old man turn us in?"

"No." I said, though perhaps it was a little too quick of an answer. "No, it's more likely that Graeves was put under surveillance after I escaped Cathedral. They have my file; they know I stayed with him when I first came to the city five years ago."

I gritted my teeth; I should have known that he'd be under some sort of surveillance, but I'd thought that after two months, they would have stopped looking in the obvious places.

"Phoenix." Xyla whispered beside me. "We need to wake the others and leave."

There was a pang in my heart; Xyla didn't know about Graeves' condition, and he'd forbidden me from saying anything. He wouldn't be able to come with us, not with his health the way it was. I simply nodded to Xyla, and we crouched back into the building, shutting the door behind us. We ran back to the apartment to warn the others.

"Gather what we need." I said. "I'll wake Kaylen and Gerimy."

"And Graeves, right?"

Another pang.

"Yes... and Graeves..."

We entered the apartment, and we found that Gerimy, Kaylen, and Graeves were already awake. The brothers were ready to leave, the old man helping them with some supplies. I blinked in surprise.

"What—"

"You had a call." Kaylen said. "Gerimy picked up the phone just a while ago."

The hair on the back of my neck stood on end at attention; it wasn't Cathedral's repertoire to call and inform targets of their situation.

Especially not black ops agents like I could only assume had been the ones to show up.

"And... the caller?" I asked.

This had the hallmarks of a close friend. The same one that had killed Brine with that head shot.

There was only one person I knew who could make a shot like that.

And one crazy enough to go down the same path I had.

"He didn't give a name." Gerimy said. "He told me to tell you we needed to get out of the building because 'they' were coming."

"More than likely, it was someone calling to lure us into a trap." Kaylen said.

"No." Mr. Graeves said, making all eyes turn to him. "That young man is someone whom I trust deeply, and I believe he's right."

"I'd say his timing to call was uncanny." Xyla said. "We've got Cathedral agents nearly ready to force us into a corner."

Mr. Graeves sighed, taking off his glasses to rub his eyes.

"Damn. I wish there had been more time." I heard him mutter.

"Sir?"

"It's nothing." Mr. Graeves said as he replaced his glasses. "You four need to go. Head for the one place they wouldn't think to look."

"Wait, what about you?" Xyla asked, stepping forward. "You're not seriously thinking about staying here, are you? They'll torture you, or worse, kill you to get the information they want."

My chest tightened a little; she was about to learn about his condition, whether or not he wanted her to. Even though I hated to admit it, I knew they wouldn't treat him with any dignity. He'd just been about to speak when coughs clawed their way out of his mouth.

First one...

Then another...

And then they were coming with such frequency that he couldn't catch his breath.

"Mr. Graeves—" I started.

"No." He coughed out before taking one of his pills; he turned to us again. "You four have to go. Now."

"But—"

Xyla began, but she was stopped by the old man as he put his hand on her head. Her eyes widened at the touch, especially when he tousled her hair a little.

"No, child." He said. "Go. You can't be caught here."

I could almost feel the pace of Xyla's rapid heartbeat. Mr. Graeves then pulled her into a hug, ducking his head down to her ear and whispering something.

And Xyla... just stood there, stiff as a board.

When Mr. Graeves pulled away, pressing his lips to her forehead, her eyes closed, twitching softly with tears. He then gave her the backpack and then turned to the three of us.

"Phoenix. Boys." He addressed us with a tone that made me immediately stand at attention. "Get her out of here."

My body sprang into action as I took her hand and led her out the door, the two brothers following behind us.

I led Xyla, Kaylen, and Gerimy down the fire escape that was the farthest from the parked vehicles of our pursuers. Kaylen insisted on scouting ahead, but I made sure that the four of us stuck together. We didn't know how many other routes they'd used to get the building, and there was no telling if they'd set up lookouts further down the road.

We had to be careful; we didn't have any weapons, and we couldn't risk gaining a vehicle or extra gear, which made the situation we were in much worse.

"What's the plan, Alpha?" Gerimy asked.

"Graeves said something about going to the one place the enemy wouldn't think to look." I said. "It's the only option we have."

The hand in mine flinched and pulled me to stop. I turned and looked at Xyla.

"Phoenix, you can't be serious!" She hissed. "We don't know what we'd be heading into!"

"She's right, Phoenix." Kaylen said, sounding equally reluctant with the plan. "We can't expect help from anyone under Joshuah's thumb."

"There *are* allies at the Den we can trust." I said, looking at Xyla. "It's worth a shot... especially now that Brine is dead."

"What do you mean?" Kaylen asked. "How can you be so sure that anyone will help us?"

"If there are survivors, they would have escaped to the Sanctuary." Xyla said. "But wouldn't Joshuah know where to find it?"

"He knows of Sanctuary, but he doesn't know the location." I reasoned.

The three of them looked like they were trying to contemplate our choices, but it was clear that we didn't have any other choice.

"Alright, so how do we get there?" Gerimy asked. "We're surrounded by cops, and we don't have any mode of transportation."

That was the only problem I hadn't thought about completely, but that didn't mean I didn't have an idea; Xyla couldn't travel the same way shifters could... but she could be carried.

The only problem with this would be what she thought about the idea. I took a deep breath and pulled my shirt off, admittedly flustering her.

"Phoenix?! What the hell are you doing?!"

"We're gonna shift." I said, dropping my shirt to the ground.

"Are you serious?!" She hissed.

"It's faster than stealing a vehicle that may or may not have a GPS tracker."

"Right, but who's going to carry me?"

"I will." I said nonchalantly. "You're my mate, so I'll take that responsibility."

She looked at me with a blank expression, her eyes blinking once, then twice as if she was processing my words.

"Is that really wise?" Kaylen asked. "Your ribs are still bruised—"

"I'm healed enough to carry my mate." I said as I looked at the eldest Crescent brother.

That one look was enough to stop him or Gerimy from saying anything else, and they stripped as well.

"Do I get a say in this?" Xyla asked.

"If you have any other idea for how to get to the Den quickly, I'm all ears, Xy." I said.

She looked at me, then the brothers, and then she sighed before kneeling to open her backpack.

"Fine. I'll take your clothes and keep them in the bag." She said.

She didn't look up as she rolled our discarded clothes and put them away. The brothers had already shifted, their transformations being nearly seamless. I took a deep breath as I started my shift; bones bowed and contorted as my skin grew thick fur.

Admittedly, it was painful because of the bruises I had, but I was able to make the change.

I forgot how much larger our wolf forms were compared to our human ones, and when Xyla stood, I had to tilt my head down to meet her eyes. She reached her hand out, and she ran her fingers through my fur.

Her touch was so comforting.

"Soft..." she muttered.

My ear twitched at the word, but I couldn't help the warm feeling in my chest. Gerimy gave a huff behind her, which earned him a snap from Kaylen.

"Am I... really going to ride on your back like you're a hellsteed?" She asked.

I bobbed my head a little and crouched to let her climb onto my back. She still looked understandably hesitant, but I let out a huff and gestured to get on.

"Alright, alright." She said, sighing as she awkwardly mounted my back, her legs curled on either side of my torso. "Let's go."

15

IMPROMPTU PLANS AND REGRETS

Xyla

MY FINGERS CURLED INTO the white fur of Phoenix's wolf form as he ran down the dark street, Kaylen and Gerimy running at his flanks. It was very odd to ride on the back of a giant wolf; I was curled into him like how I would ride my motorcycle.

And to be honest, it was a very similar feeling, the wind tousling my hair and the same adrenaline I felt.

I looked behind us as the low-income housing building grew smaller in the distance and eventually became a part of the shadowy cityscape.

There was still so much I wanted to know about Mr. Graeves.

About him and my mother.

I knew even less about her.

I wished I could have asked him more about her, about me and my sister.

'But... where would I even start...?' I wondered. 'What question would I ask them first?'

About their relationship?

About her reasoning for giving us up?

About her vision and what it meant?

I shook my head of such distracting thoughts and turned my head forward as Phoenix and the brothers diverged from the road we'd been on.

The glimpse of a Cathedral patrol vehicle told me all I needed to know as we ducked into an alleyway. The wolves crouched, and I leaned in closer to Phoenix as the vehicle drove by, their searchlight missing us just barely.

"That was way too close." I muttered.

Phoenix gave a huff, seeming to agree with me.

We waited until the street was quiet again, and when the coast was clear, the wolves padded down the street.

'Traveling like this is getting more and more dangerous...' I thought with narrowed eyes as I looked around. 'Anyone could spot us out here in the open like this.'

We'd just entered Downtown; while it wasn't as populated as the innermost parts of the city, the risk was still high.

"You three should shift back." I said, looking at the wolves. "Anyone would be suspect of three shifted wolves and a woman with Mesmer eyes."

Perhaps a lot of this trouble could have been avoided if I'd invested in color contacts to hide my eyes. Well, I guess hindsight is twenty-twenty.

Phoenix gave another huff and bobbed his head. We ducked into another alley where he let me down from his back, and I knelt to unzip my backpack.

I didn't look at the sounds of bones and joints popping in and out of place filled the alley as they shifted back into their human forms.

"We'll need another mode of transportation if we want to make it to the Den." Phoenix said with a sigh as I handed him and the brothers back their clothes.

Gerimy scoffed at our current plan.

"I still can't believe you want to go back there." He said. "We barely made it out the last time, and you want to go back? Why?"

"He's got a point." Kaylen said with a sigh. "Not to mention the fact that Joshuah will have a kill-on-sight order on you."

I looked at Phoenix as a thick silence hung over the alleyway, his brow furrowed in deep thought. There was a glimmer of realization in his eyes.

"Joshuah didn't earn the mantle." He said after a moment. "I gave it to him, but his hold is not absolute."

"We know that. That's why everyone responded to your Call back then." Gerimy said as he pulled his shirt down. "What does that have to do with anything?"

"What exactly are you planning, Phoenix?" I asked as I looked at him, readjusting the backpack on my shoulder.

The look in Phoenix's eyes told me everything before he'd even could say anything; I wondered if this was an instinct that came with the Bond we shared.

The thrum reverberated with a feeling of uncertainty, the deep thoughts of a risk that didn't need to be taken.

"If Joshuah truly wants my title as Alpha," he said, standing tall with pride; "then he'll have to challenge me for it."

I could only stare at him in confusion; what the hell did that even mean?!

Mr. Graeves

With Xyla, Phoenix, and those others gone, I could let myself deteriorate in peace. My illness was sapping my strength; I found it remarkable that my body hadn't failed completely while they were there, that I'd even lasted as long as I did before they came.

I could only guess that my ancestors had something planned for me, and that something was to see at least one of our daughters alive and strong.

And she certainly was strong.

Xyla Coltt was strong and ambitious, much like I had been when I was her age. And she was much stronger than she knew. I saw the tears in the sheets on her bed; if my beloved was right—as she always seemed to be—then Xyla and Areena were more than just Mesmers. They would get stronger in their abilities, and they might gain even more before the time came for them to fight one another.

Gods, I hoped they didn't have to go through with this. I wanted so badly for her vision to change.

It was getting harder for me to breathe, and the dryness in my mouth tasted coppery.

I was sitting in my recliner, my strength having left me. I half-wished that I could numb the pain and put myself to sleep where I could fade away, but there was half of me that thought it foolish.

I still had one wish left, and I was stubbornly keeping myself alive for no other reason than spite.

"You're still so stubborn, my love."

My old heart skipped a beat at the bell-like voice, and breath sucked into my lungs. I turned my head towards the sound, and there she stood.

A woman with long white hair, pale skin, and those marble like eyes I loved so much.

"E-Elita..." I rasped, immediately regretting it when my cough started up again.

Her pale hand gently took my trembling one as she knelt at my side.

"Shhh, my darling empath." She soothed as she brought my hand to her cheek. "I would not let you be alone during these last moments."

Her cyan blue eyes were as calm as an ocean lagoon, and yet they were misty with tears.

I hated to see her cry; she was too kind a soul to be plagued by such sorrow.

"I saw her..." I whispered, gently squeezing her hand, though it was a weak squeeze. "I saw our daughter."

There was a sad smile on her pale lips as she nodded.

"Indeed." She said. "She has your stubborn spirit, my love."

"And your strong will." I chuckled a little, trying not to cough more.

I took a deep breath, only for my chest to wheeze as it rose and fell.

"Has... has your vision changed at all?" I asked, struggling to speak through the ever-increasing pain.

The woman gently traced the wrinkled flesh of my hand as she looked at me.

"My visions are always changing, Oliver." She said, that sad smile still on her lips. "But... my vision of the twins... it has not changed all that much. Nothing... except for an additional detail..."

My heart hammered in my chest, giving me a startled cough, and she gently stroked my cheek to calm me.

"W-What have you seen, Elita?"

She was silent for a long time, and then her lips parted.

"The bloodlines of the Morning Star and the Last *Aster-Blood*..." she whispered, leaning in close as if she were afraid someone would hear; "they shall converge once more and a child will be born."

My eyes widened, my vision becoming blurry with tears.

I had so many questions.

Which one would have the child?

Did the child's conception decide the victor at all?

What about Areena?

If the child was hers, then would *that* man be the father?!

The revelation and fear worried me more than anything, especially now that I couldn't do anything about it.

My failing body was my tolling bell; I'd run out of time.

"E-Elita..." I wheezed. "I-I—"

"Shhhhh," she soothed, her tears becoming more and more apparent; "shhh, shhh, my darling Oliver Graeves."

Her other hand gently stroked my cheek, her thumb wiping the tears that trickled from my crow's feet.

"Our grandchild will live." She whispered. "*She* will live surrounded by a family that will love and care for her."

I let out a breath of relief, and my body felt like it was floating; her words told me everything I needed to know, and the only worry I had was of Areena and her fate.

Was she still destined to be that man's puppet, his weapon?

"I wish…" I muttered, my breaths becoming slow as my limbs slowly lost their feeling; I could barely feel her touch anymore. "I-I wish… that she… that they both knew…"

"I know, my love." She whispered, her voice cracking with her heartfelt sorrow. "They both will know before the Time comes."

It was a promise I wished I could have kept, but as I sat in that recliner, my body was becoming cold; I knew I couldn't keep it.

But *she* could.

"Look… after them…" I forced the words out as darkness danced at the edges of my vision. "Please…"

Her pale lips moved, but I couldn't hear her words.

But I could read them.

I felt at peace; I'd been able to do the thing I wished.

I got to see her again.

Her.

The lovely Elita.

The Oracle of Cathedral.

My forbidden lover.

The mother of Xyla and Areena.

The last of her noble bloodline.

Elita Adalaine Morgenstern.

16

RETURN TO THE DEN

Xyla

ODDLY ENOUGH, THE DEN wasn't as teeming with security as we initially thought it would be. In fact, there didn't even seem to be a regular patrol at the perimeter. It was as if Joshuah's forces had been cut in half and then cut in half again; the numbers were far fewer than before.

I wasn't the only one who thought something was off.

"It's strange." Kaylen muttered. "You'd think with our escape, Joshuah would have beefed up security."

"And it's a ghost town." I said.

"You'd think that whatever alliance Joshuah made with Cathedral would have left him with soldiers and weapons." Gerimy said. "What's going on here?"

"I'm not sure." Phoenix said. "But I don't think Joshuah is the one in control of all of this. He's just a pawn in this."

I looked at him with a raised eyebrow; I could see what would make him think that, and it made sense.

"Someone wanted to control the Pack, and they saw him as someone they could easily manipulate." I said. "Considering how narrow-minded your brother is, he was the perfect target. Much offense meant."

"Yeah, you certainly have that part right." Phoenix chuckled wryly, though he wasn't smiling along with it. "Joshuah has never been one for strategy or free thinking. That lack of initiative has been the disgrace that's led to his downfall."

Phoenix seemed a little more into the leadership role than I thought he would be. Whatever he was planning, he certainly had set his mind to it.

Gods, I just hoped he actually had a plan.

I looked back at the dismal forces held by our enemy. The more I thought about what Phoenix had said, the more plausible it seemed; it definitely seemed like something from *that man's* repertoire when it came to controlling people.

'He wants control over the Black Wing Group, the Pack... but why?' I wondered. 'What could that man want with groups that are considerably smaller than Cathedral or the Rising? And Areena... why manipulate her into being an active participant?'

I remembered what Mr. Graeves had said about the prophecy, and I wondered what *that man* had learned about Seraphim.

I gritted my teeth and looked at the gate; we wouldn't get any answers just staying on the outskirts.

"Could we get through the woods to the Sanctuary?" I asked. "You guys know this place better than I do."

"They could be patrolling the woods." Kaylen said. "Very few people actually know how to get Sanctuary. Joshuah would have patrols near the woods to scout out the entrance."

"Then we came here for nothing?!" Gerimy nearly screeched.

"Quiet!" I hissed, and then I looked at the young Alpha beside me. "Your choice, Phoenix. What do we do?"

He looked at me and then at the sparsely guarded gate. His brow furrowed in deep thought, and he was silent for a moment or two. He then gave an exhale, which sounded more like an exasperated sigh.

"There... is another way inside..." he said. "But... it's not very pleasant..."

Before any of us could ask, Phoenix turned and walked the opposite way of the Den's entrance. Kaylen and Gerimy visibly shuddered in disgust before following. I blinked, confused and out of the loop, and then I followed the three wolf-shifters to whatever route Phoenix had in mind.

Turns out, the alternate route to infiltrate the Den was indeed unpleasant, but I'd honestly faced much worse. The route in question was an underground tunnel that was akin to a sewage drain. I descended the cool metal ladder behind Phoenix, and the musky scent of sewage stung at my sense of smell.

"How do you know we won't be found this way?" I asked as I looked into the shadows at Phoenix's silhouette.

His hazel eyes were glowing gold in the dark, and he held out his hand to me. I took his hand as I found my footing on the damp concrete floor.

"In all honesty," he said, "I don't. But this route was once used for scent tracking drills for young recruits a few generations back."

"Yeah, and it was also a punishment for those who failed a task during basic training." Gerimy said, fighting the urge to gag as he covered his nose.

"Since our father's death, no one has used it."

I raised an eyebrow and looked at Phoenix.

"Wait, the Pack has a militant branch?" I asked.

I knew that there had been some beefed up security during the month we'd stayed at the Den, but it didn't seem to be equipped to be a militant outfit.

"The Pack *is* a militant branch." Kaylen said. "Or it had been a very long time ago."

"Generations ago," Phoenix elaborated, "the Den was an armed security service, a reserve for the forces that served the Council. My grandfather was once a soldier. He tried for years to rebuild that reputation, to keep us relevant. And it drove him to an early grave... and my father certainly didn't make good on that ambition with his alcohol problem."

"But why isn't the Den still part of armed security?" I asked.

"Because of widespread discrimination." Kaylen said. "No one really knows who started the Separation, but when shifters started being denied rights, they all fell back to the community of the Den for support."

"And the Den became a world whole and unto itself." Phoenix finished, a tone of distaste clear in the somber voice he spoke in.

There was silence in the tunnels after the heavy explanation, and Gerimy groaned.

"Well, that was a history lesson that I'm pretty sure I didn't need."

"You're lucky it's dark, or I'd smack you upside the head." Kaylen said in a disapproving tone. "Pay attention to your lessons!"

"Anyway," Phoenix sighed, gently squeezing my hand while using his other to feel along the wall; "my father put me and Joshuah through that same training, and it's because of that training that I was able to rise through the ranks in the Tracker Division in Cathedral."

There was a slight bristle to his tone, and I recalled the abuse that he and Joshuah had gone through as children at the hands of their father. It was odd to compare the two brothers, how their paths diverged when they both went through the same harrowing experiences.

'Almost similar to me and my sister...'

"It is different from you and Areena." Luka's voice echoed. *"You two were separated after the orphanage fire. You both grew up in different environments."*

In my gut, I knew he was right; we had grown up differently, and I realized how easily it could have been that our roles could have been reversed.

That I could have been manipulated by *that man* and Areena grew up with Luka.

'I wish you could have raised her, too, Luka...'

He didn't answer, but I really didn't have to hear one from him. I looked at Phoenix, or as well I could in the dark. I could vaguely make out his silhouette.

'Mr. Graeves was there for him when he left the Den, took him in and got him the job at Cathedral.' I hummed to myself. 'I'm grateful for that.'

As my thoughts went to the old man — about my blood father — my chest tightened; I wished so much that we could have talked more.

There was still so much I wanted to ask.

So much to apologize for...

'Maybe after all this, I'll visit him again...'

I had to bite back a scoff at my own thoughts.

After all this, huh...

I recalled Phoenix's plan for regaining control of the Pack; he was going to challenge Joshuah for the mantle of Alpha.

I shouldn't have felt nervous; the stubborn wolf-shifter had survived a battle with me and whatever had driven me to act like a savage animal in the Pit. He could survive this fight with his brother.

But... for some reason, the thought of it all made my heartbeat throb in my ears.

"You're nervous." Phoenix whispered, drawing me from my thoughts. "That's not like you."

"I am *not* nervous." I huffed. "I just don't know why you have to fight for a title that you technically never gave away in the first place."

"It's more than just a fight, Xy." He answered with a tone of exhaustion. "The mantle wasn't formally given to my brother, but he could still lead everyone until the Pack heard my Call. Right now, no one is Alpha, and the Pack is divided. This battle will unite the two factions before a civil war can start."

The politics and traditions of wolf-shifters had always been so odd to me; even though one of the men who had raised me was part of a Pack, I never learned the formalities. I regretted not having asked in my youth.

"What will this fight prove, exactly?" I asked. "What's the point of doing all this?"

"This fight will decide who has the strength to be Alpha, as well as the drive." He said. "And... normally, it would be a battle of submission. The first to surrender would be the one to lose."

"Wait, that's not the case now?" I asked.

"No..." He said. "Joshuah wouldn't abide by that tradition... because I'm *technically* a deserter, this battle... will be different..."

I didn't like where this was going; I had a good feeling about what he meant.

"So... that means—"

"It'll be a fight to the death." Phoenix nodded his head solemnly. "Single combat in our wolf forms."

The stakes were high, and his words only added to the gravity of the situation. Even with his reasoning at the next move, whether or not it was logical, it didn't escape me that he seemed hesitant.

'Is he doubting his resolve?' I wondered. 'Is he really capable of killing his brother?'

I realized it was *this* that I was worried about: Phoenix didn't seem the type to kill, even if he needed to.

And this plan of his was putting himself at war with his own moral compass.

Phoenix gently squeezed my hand, as if he could read my thoughts and confirm them with such a silent gesture.

"Phoenix—"

"This is our way up." He spoke, stopping the four of us.'

I heard the subtle *thump* of his hand as he took hold of another ladder, and then he let go of my hand to start his climb. The shadowy air was filled with more muffled *thumps* and *clinks* as he went up the ladder. The light of dawn was breaking overhead, becoming a dull spotlight as Phoenix removed the hole cover. I looked at Kaylen and Gerimy before I climbed to the surface. I rubbed my eyes at the light, and I was met with an orange-pink colored sky that faded to the light blue of the horizon of day.

17

THE TRIALS OF LEXISHIRA, PART TWO

Lexy

I DIDN'T DARE MOVE from my seat, not with that stupid fake leader I'd once been forced to call my partner sitting across from me. Joshuah was forcing me to play along with his little charade of house, and I felt all the more repulsed by it.

I knew why he was doing it; he was trying to get my composure to break.

Waiting for me to tell him the name of my *animae nexum* so that he could kill him.

"Come now, my dear." He said with a sickening smirk. "You must eat. You have yourself and another to take care of now, after all."

He was toying with me, eating so sloppily from a large plate of food while I was given a much smaller portion.

And it was food that I couldn't eat while I was pregnant: par cooked mackerel, chicken salad with brie cheese, and orange juice.

The sight and smell of the fish made bile steep in my stomach.

This room was a prison cell, and this was one of his many forms of torture. He would deny me necessities, such as clean clothes and comfortable pillows. I could only bathe in water, no soap or shampoo.

It was a miracle my baby was still alive despite all of this.

Noticing my discomfort at the food set in front of me, Joshua smirked and wiped his mouth.

"Come now, *Lexishira*—"

"*Don't* call me that." I hissed at him, fighting the urge to shift and snap his neck in my teeth.

But I couldn't shift, not with my baby almost to term.

Wolf-shifter pregnancies were shorter compared to those of humans, around two-and-a-half to three months.

All I could do was fight back with my words; they were my most prized weapon, after all.

The man in front of me—the impudent rat who was trying to play Alpha—gave a sigh, and he leaned against his hand.

"You know, Lexy," he said with a childish pout, "I try to do right by you. Why must you act like such a misbehaved little pup?"

"Do right by me?" I asked with a scoff. "You've done nothing but made me uncomfortable since you moved me here. You give me food that you know I can't eat a lot of. You've stripped me of basic rights. What do you think warrants I be grateful for anything?"

"But isn't this better than being in that stuffy basement of prisoners?" He asked. "No doubt that corpse has made several of those rats get sick and die themselves."

"Gods, you are insufferable." I said. "You're no leader, and the actions you took to play one are incorrigible. You killed Sareena and drove your own brother away from the Pack—"

"My brother is weak!" Joshuah snarled, his teeth gritting with childish jealousy. "He let himself feel guilty for the death of a woman who wasn't even his mate!"

"You knew Phoenix rules himself by his moral code, and *that* is why he's a better leader than you."

The man's fingers flexed and relaxed in a futile attempt to calm his temper.

He was losing it.

"*I* am the Alpha! Me!" He roared, sweeping everything off the table in front of us in his tantrum. "While Phoenix was off feeling sorry for himself, I was the one keeping things together here!"

Any normal person would have flinched at his outburst, his true colors of inferiority and jealousy on display, but I didn't move a muscle. It didn't stop the smug smile that tugged at my lips.

No matter how hard I pushed his buttons, he couldn't hurt me; it was taboo to lay a hand on a pregnant she-wolf.

"You made a deal with the devil, Joshuah." I said. "I believe that's how the saying goes. You sold out your brother and the Pack for your own pride. You're nothing but a coward—"

Slap!

The sound echoed off the walls in that room, and pain bloomed across my cheek. There was a coppery taste in my mouth, and I felt sick to my stomach.

He slapped me.

The stupid fucker actually slapped me!

Joshuah's nails, threatening to sharpen into claws, dug into my scalp as he grabbed my hair and forced me to look at him.

His eyes were wild, and he looked like he was nearly rabid, foaming at the mouth in his rage.

"Don't think that Tradition protects a traitorous bitch like you, *Lexishira*." He growled dangerously. "Remember, I *can* force that child out prematurely."

I spat blood into his eye, making him recoil. I finally stood from my chair, grabbing a fork and scratching it across his cheek.

"*Long live the Alpha, Phoenix Bryte!*" I declared as his devoted lackeys came in. "*Long live Phoenix Bryte and Xyla Coltt!*"

"A-Alpha Joshuah—!"

"Don't worry about me!" He snapped at them. "Kill her, Gods damn it!"

The lackeys, however, didn't move.

They knew the law and Tradition; I couldn't be harmed because of my baby, and I had every right to defend myself, whether I was a prisoner or not.

Even if my attacker was the *supposed* leader.

"Your *Alpha* slapped me." I said. "He laid a hand on a pregnant she-wolf!"

The two men were in shock, and despite Joshuah's orders to kill me, they couldn't, lest they commit taboo themselves.

"All of you are fucking useless!" Joshuah roared as he stormed out of the room, holding his face where the fork had scratched him. "Lock this door! Starve her out!"

Slam!

The door shut, and Joshuah kept shouting down the hallway.

"Find the traitor and his whore!" I heard him scream. "And find that woman's two brat siblings!"

My chest tightened at those words, and my tongue welled in my throat.

I knew whom he'd meant; he was talking about Kaylen and Gerimy.

'He's going to kill my brothers?!'

He was going to kill them... and I couldn't do anything.

I was a prisoner in this place that had once been my home. I put my hand on my swollen belly, feeling the baby within still moving.

I prayed to the Gods' Tree and Lady Arboriah Lux, praying for their safety.

I knew I couldn't survive off of prayer alone. I looked at the discarded food on the floor. The food I'd been given was food I couldn't eat while pregnant, but Joshuah's food was safe.

He'd been pigging out on roasted chicken, steamed vegetables, and roasted potatoes.

I was glad then that I'd been locked in that room. I slowly knelt to the ground, careful of my belly, and I ate the food from the floor.

I didn't have time to care about my dignity or my pride.

I had to survive.

For my baby in my belly.

For my *animae nexum*, Jaye Hazelle.

For the survivors who'd escaped the chaotic rebellion.

For Kaylen and Gerimy, my dear brothers and the only family I had left.

For Phoenix Bryte, the true Alpha of the Pack, and his mate, the Mesmer, Xyla Coltt.

18

THE HORRORS AFTER THE BATTLE

Phoenix

WE QUICKLY DISCOVERED WHAT the Den's security was lacking: there were hardly any people in the compound at all. The once clean and manicured streets of the town were in shambles, rubbish and clumps of overturned dirt littering the sidewalk. Windows were cracked or completely shattered.

"This place turned into a battle zone." Xyla muttered beside me. "I wonder how many people could make it out."

I didn't have the heart to speak an answer; while there were no corpses on the streets, there was the smell of death in the air. No matter how hopeful I was, I knew people had died in this battle.

"Celia made it out." Kaylen said. "I can still feel her side of the Bond."

That much was actually a relief; Celia was a civilian, not a soldier, and that meant that there might have been a good number of survivors from the battle.

When we rounded the corner that led to the square, I froze in place, my blood running cold and anger boiling in the pit of my stomach at the same time. I felt Xyla walk into my back, and I held my arm out to stop her from coming around that fateful corner.

"Phoenix—?"

"Don't look."

She sighed and pushed my arm away.

"Geez, Phoenix will you..."

She trailed off when she saw what had made me stop, and her eyes widened in shock. I couldn't stop Kaylen or Gerimy when they rounded the corner, and the youngest grit his teeth.

"That bastard!"

In the square were three make-shift crosses, hanging from chains tied around their wrists and the torsos, were three men. They'd been beaten and bruised, bloodied from the gashes across their bodies. Their yellowish-gray decomposing skin was blotted in deep bluish-purple spots where the blood had been cut off from circulation and congealed. Flies buzzed around rotten openings where carrion birds had poked through and feasted on the organs. And to add more to the disrespect, there was a sign hanging from each of their necks. In black paint were the words *"Death to all Traitors."*

"What the fuck?" Xyla breathed, her hands clenched tight.

Kaylen raked his fingers through his hair.

"What has he done?" He said. "This... this is taboo..."

He looked like he was on the verge of a mental and an emotional breakdown at the same time. Gerimy, on the other hand, was seething with rage.

"That fucking bastard!" He growled, his body shaking as if he was going to shift on the spot. "I'm gonna rip that damn psychopath's throat out with my—"

"No." I said as I stepped forward. "No, Joshuah is mine to handle. My mess to clean up."

"Phoenix..." Xyla muttered as she looked at me.

I was caught between grief and vengeance. I knew those three men; they were brothers I'd made during my father's hellacious training. Each of them had families.

Wives, life partners, and children.

Those families had suffered a much unnecessary loss, all because my brother was spiraling out of control.

Suddenly, I was pulled by the arm, and I looked at Xyla. She pulled me behind the wall and poked her finger into my chest.

"You can't let your anger get the better of you here." She said. "I know that you're angry. Trust me; I can feel it. But you can't let yourself get tunnel vision."

In all honesty, I was so shocked by her words that I forgot my rage; she'd matured a lot in such a short time, and I was proud of her for that.

But I knew that there was more to it; she was speaking from experience. She'd avenged Luka in a rage after he'd been killed. She gently reached out and put her hand on my cheek.

"Mind your head, okay?" She said, running her thumb under my eye.

I let out a breath, and I touched my forehead to hers. I admired how calm she was.

No, it was more than that: she *was* angry, but she wasn't letting it get to her.

A thought came to mind that brought a smile to my lips.

'She'll make an amazing Luna.'

I pulled away from her, nodding to thank her for her rational mind.

"Not to disturb your little bonding moment here, but can we get back to the problem at hand—ow!"

Kaylen had hit Gerimy over the head, scolding him for not being respectful.

"No, Gerimy has a point." I said, looking around the corner at the warning. "We can't be caught here."

"Joshuah must have the rest of whatever forces he has patrolling the House." Xyla said. "He'll have kept the prisoners close by, knowing how paranoid he is."

That fact only made me more worried for Lexy; she must have been two months pregnant by now, and the stress couldn't be helping her condition.

"Agreed. He'd want to keep a close eye on them." I said. "Especially Lexy."

I held my tongue; the brothers didn't know about Lexy finding her *animae nexum* or that she was pregnant. Telling them would only make them want to charge the Alpha House, and it would only lead to their deaths.

"Why would he need to keep an eye on Lexy?" Kaylen asked. "He might be obsessed with her, but surely he wouldn't show any favoritism... would he?"

I looked at the brothers, their brows furrowed in confusion. I sighed; there was no keeping the secret now. I knew the brothers would continue to ask questions now that I'd let it slip.

"Joshuah... might use her as bait to lure out Jaye..."

I said, looking at them.

Kaylen's eyes widened while the younger Crescent brother just looked all the more confused.

"What does that Investigator have to do with our sister?" Gerimy asked, apparently still not getting it.

"Because—"

"Lexy and that Investigator are *animae nexum*." Kaylen said.

"And... there's more..." I continued. "Lexy... is pregnant with Jaye's child..."

We couldn't stay in that place for long, seeing as we didn't know what patrols were out. As we moved through the compound and retreated to the forest, Kaylen and Gerimy were still trying to come to terms with the news of Lexy's condition.

"She found her *animae nexum*, and she didn't tell us?!" Kaylen hissed. "What was she thinking?! We could have helped!"

"Why did it have to be that Investigator?" Gerimy grumbled. "He's a vampire!"

"*That's* what you're worried about, Gerimy? Really?!" Kaylen scolded.

"Either way," Xyla said, breaking up the brothers; "this news changes things. We already knew that we need to free the captive rebels before your big showdown against Joshuah."

"And we need to figure out how many were captured." Kaylen said. "Those three dead soldiers were a warming to these who escaped, but we have no clue how many captives there are."

"Or how many he's killed besides those three." Xyla sighed. "And how exactly are we going to execute any plan when we have no base of operations, and it's only the four of us?" Gerimy asked, crossing his arms. "It's us against an army, even if it is meager."

"No." Xyla said. "The remnants of an army. Didn't you see? Those patrols we saw only had Pack members. No Black Wings or Cathedral agents."

Kaylen's eyes widened a little, and he crossed his arms, holding his chin in thought.

"She's right." He said. "The only ones we've seen are those loyal to Joshuah."

"Why would Cathedral extract their forces from the Alpha House?" Gerimy asked.

"To look for us." I realized, remembering Mr. Graeves' words. "They wouldn't think to look for us here when we escaped before."

"Realistically, Vanguard Hollum would have tried to absorb any Black Wing members into the Rising." Xyla sighed as she leaned against a tree. "The bastard's been all too eager to take down any groups that oppose his. It would be a goal they'd be happy to achieve with Brine dead."

"And any survivors from the uprising would have fled to the Sanctuary to wait out Joshuah's crumbling rule." I said.

"So, if we can find Sanctuary again, we'll find the survivors and begin to actually come up with a plan for all of this." Xyla added.

"This little back-and-forth theorizing thing between you both is uber creepy." Gerimy said, grunting when Kaylen elbowed him in the ribs.

"So, how do we find Sanctuary?" Kaylen asked, turning to Xyla. "Lexy and Celia brought you there. Do you remember how to get there?"

Xyla had been about to say something when branches rustled behind us. We all turned on our heels to see a familiar girl with long black hair peeking from behind a tree.

"Celia…" Kaylen muttered, his voice sounding relieved.

The girl popped into the open as tears formed in her eyes.

"Kaylen!" She called out as she ran towards the oldest brother, jumping into his arms and wrapping her arms around his neck and her legs around his waist.

"Celia, are the others okay?" I asked, hope sparkling at the thought of Lexy being among the survivors.

The dark-haired girl looked at me, and then at Xyla, and her eyes widened. Kaylen let her down as he turned to her as well.

"Luna Xyla!" She called out. "Everyone! Our Alpha and Luna have returned!"

The trees rustled around our small group, and people emerged. There were wolf-shifters — some from the Pack and others from the Black Wing Group, I assumed — and there were also vampires of varying generations. They murmured when they looked at Xyla, and I instinctively stepped in front of her.

"Young Xyla." A familiar voice addressed my mate, and I turned to see a familiar mop of sandy blonde hair.

"Avery." Xyla addressed him, putting her hand on my shoulder. "You've done as you've promised."

I looked at her over my shoulder, confused to what she meant, and the man called Avery nodded, putting his fist to his chest.

"Yes, ma'am." He said. "Though, not quite as I hoped."

Others followed the salute.

The salute to a leader.

"It's fine, Avery." She said. "Brine had no clue that you were the one I'd left affairs to. He just assumed her was the leader."

I blinked, staring between the two of them as they spoke. Gerimy seemed to be just as confused.

"Okay, what the hell?" He said. "Who is the guy?"

Xyla and Avery turned to look at us, and she smiled softly.

"Everyone, this is Avery Malcolm," Xyla introduced, "my successor as leader of the Black Wings."

It was in that moment I realized just how Xyla's mind worked; she'd expected this, of that, I was sure.

19

THE TRUTH ABOUT XYLA

Xyla

AVERY LED US AND his small patrol back to the Sanctuary, or rather, one of the many entrances to it, apparently. I looked at Celia, who was riding on Kaylen's back.

"This is different from the entrance Lex brought us to the first time." I pointed out.

"It's an old escape route." Avery answered, bringing my attention back to him. "After our retreat, we sealed the entrance, and we made sure there was quite an audience for it."

"You made it seem like all the escaped rebels died in the cave-in?" Kaylen asked. "That was exceptionally risky. You could have collapsed the whole subterranean structure."

"We knew the rebellion would have been a long shot." Avery said. "Luckily, a few Pack members were willing to help us 'die' and get Joshuah off our backs."

"So we do have allies that are still in Joshua's service?" Phoenix asked.

"Yes, though, given the circumstances, we've not gotten any other information from them about the people he has captured."

We arrived at one of the larger halls, and we saw just how much Avery and the rebels had done. Small children were making the most of the situation while older ones were helping to distribute food.

I was astonished.

Every family had a space and food.

Wolf-shifters and vampires were coexisting, surviving in such dismal circumstances.

Other Black Wings members, half-witches and half-demons alike, were being excepted by the Pack.

'This... is just like what you wanted the world to be like Luka.' My chest tightened. 'Your dream...'

"We evacuated many of the non-combatants as possible." Avery said. "Though we still have many missing."

"Joshuah's prisoners, you mean." Phoenix said. "What about Lexy? Is she here?"

We didn't know if Lexy was captive or not, but with her condition, I had a feeling what the answer would be. Avery sighed and shook his head.

"No." He said. "Young Celia had certainly been upset about it. I understand that she's pregnant."

"Yes." Phoenix said, nodding a little. "And that's what we've been worried about, too."

"We know she'd being held with the other rebels." A black-haired man said. "But we don't know her status beyond that."

His name was Brohm Grover, one of my lieutenants that I'd left to lead alongside Avery. He didn't give off the scent of a typical wolf-shifter; his blue-green eyes were a giveaway that he was a rarity.

He was a wolf-shifter without a wolf form, basically a human. The scars he had told a story of abuse, no doubt at the hands of his family, abused just because he couldn't shift into a wolf form. Luka and Avery had brought him into the group; I'd first met him when I was twelve years old.

"They've also fortified the Alpha House." Avery nodded. "The rebellion's first attack put a dent in what minor forces he'd been able to muster, and now the coward has locked himself inside. The staff of the House are his hostages."

"Do we have a list of those who are captured or dead?" I asked.

Avery nodded, and a list was handed to me via Brohm. Phoenix was watching me as I scanned the paper, and I couldn't help but narrow my eyes at the number of names. Knowing what I did about Joshuah, I knew he had killed several of them. I folded the paper with a sigh and tapped to Phoenix's chest. He was staring at me, and I raised an eyebrow at him.

"Phoenix." I whispered. "Earth to Phoenix."

He jolted a little and took the paper.

"S-Sorry." He said.

Out of the corner of my eye, I noticed Avery bite back a smirk. I had a feeling of what Phoenix was thinking while he was staring at me, and something told me that Avery had an inkling too.

"There's a room that you and Bryte can use to rest." Avery said. "I know that your journey's been a long one."

I'd wondered why he'd said it like that, but I realized that there were two reasons: Kaylen would slay with Celia — Gerimy would probably tag along there — and he *knew* Phoenix was my *animae nexum*.

In all honesty, it probably wasn't hard to deduce, given how he acted around me.

"We'll wait until you've rested to come up with a plan of attack." Brohm said. "You're our leader—"

"No." I said, looking at my former lieutenant with a sad smile. "Avery is your leader, and you are the second-in-command."

"Be that as it may," Avery chuckled, stepping forward to put a hand on my shoulder, "you are the one that Luka had so much faith in. You are the reason we're called the Black Wing Group."

Avery's hand gently squeezed my shoulder, and it was an odd comfort to me; he and Luka both believed in me because of the mark on my shoulder, and looking back, it raised a lot of questions.

'What *exactly* did they know about that mark?' I wondered. 'And how did they know about it?'

I'd never asked them when I was younger, and I somewhat regretted not asking them anything about what they knew.

I put his hand on and looked at him.

"After a bit... could we talk?"

Avery's lips twitched into a sad smile, and that subconsciously answered one of my questions. He nodded.

"Of course." He said. "We'll talk when you're ready."

I bit my tongue as I nodded, and Avery pressed a kiss against my forehead. As he led Phoenix and me to the room we'd be using, my heart wanted nothing more than to reach out to the man that had been my other brother and, many times, was a father like Luka had been.

'I'm ready now...'

The room was similar to a private quarters room; I'd had one at the Group's compound before I left. It didn't have much, but it did have a bed, a desk, and a vanity with an antique wash basin. I set my backpack down and sat on the edge of the bed, letting my head hang with a sigh.

"Xy?"

I looked up at Phoenix as he knelt in front of me, putting his warm hands on my cheeks.

"You okay?"

I gave him a sad smile as I leaned against his hands.

"Yeah... I guess..." I sighed. "I'm... just not sure where to start..."

"What do you mean?" He asked.

"Well, I do sort of owe you an explanation." I said. "That entire experience must have been confusing..."

"It was a bit, yes." He said. "I wasn't going to push it, though."

I chuckled softly and took a deep breath; he needed to know.

"Avery and Luka were *animae nexum*." I said. "They both took me in after the orphanage fire. It was a... unique experience, to say the least. A wolf-shifter and a vampire, also adding the fact that it was a homosexual relationship, you can imagine the hate they both got for it."

I remembered how Brine would get in trouble at school for getting into fights with other kids who called Luka a faggot and other slurs. Brine might have grown up to be a self-centered prick with a superiority complex, but he was a kid with a big heart back then.

"In truth, they weren't the only questionable relationship in the Outskirts, and it wasn't the only issue." I said. "People in the Outskirts were still being treated as dirt and shit. It was like nothing had changed since Arboriah Lux's Reformation. That was when Luka and Avery started their equal rights movement."

"And, you became the Group's symbol?" Phoenix asked.

"Well, yes and no." I said as I sat back on the bed. "When Luka was killed... the ones involved in the movement were scared for their lives. Many thought of putting it all behind them, going back to probably worse conditions than before. Even Avery was losing faith after he died; he had lost a part of himself, after all."

I clenched my fists, my fingers curling into the thin blankets covering the bed.

"I was beyond pissed." I said. "They followed Luka because he'd given them hope, and when he died, they were going to disgrace him further by running away and ignoring the problem."

"So... you took matters into your own hands..." Phoenix said. "You avenged Luka's death by putting that cop in the hospital."

I flinched a little when he brought that up; there was something else about that incident that wasn't in my records at Cathedral. I cleared my throat a little.

"*Ahem...* there was something else about it..." I said. "Even Avery doesn't know about it... well, he might know about it now..."

Phoenix gently took my hand.

"You don't have to tell—"

"I accidentally used my ability on him." I blurted out.

Phoenix's hand squeezed mine a bit; I think it was more of a flinch rather than a comforting gesture.

"I thought you said you've never used your ability..."

"No, I said that I try not to use it." I said. "After what happened... I was so scared..."

"What happened...?"

I looked at him; he was still trying to be supportive and understand what I was going through.

"I confronted the cop... I told him off, that I wanted him to experience the same pain and suffering I did when he took Luka away from me and my family... and then he..."

"So, he was the one who hurt himself..." He said. "You never laid a hand on him."

"I tried to stop him... but I couldn't..." I bowed my head a little.

Phoenix pulled me into a hug, gently running his fingers through my hair.

"It's alright." He whispered. "It's alright."

I let him hold me for a while before I composed myself, or rather, as well as I could; I needed to tell Phoenix the truth about everything.

He deserved that much.

"I took up Luka's cause after that." I muttered. "After the news had gotten out about the cop being put in the hospital, they somehow made the connection that I'd been the one to put him there, and they all began to have hope again. I was still young, not even a month after my nineteenth birthday."

"How did Avery become the leader of the Group?" He asked.

"After the Morgenstern Place shooting, I told Avery and Brohm about what I'd seen. Avery knew I had a twin sister; though, he thought it very unlikely that the person I'd seen had actually been Areena." I said. "I told Avery that I couldn't get the Group involved, not after the incident. I told him to make up whatever excuse would sound reasonable concerning my absence.... and I left..."

"And Brine...?"

"I... asked Avery and Brohm to humor him." I hesitated to say so, but it was the truth. "It was an error in judgment on my part. I should have known that the bratty bastard would look for me."

"Was he really that obsessed with you?" Phoenix asked.

I could tell by the bite in his tone that he didn't like the behavior we'd both seen.

"Brine was already acting like a radical, even before Luka's passing." I sighed. "Seeing as how Luka always doted on me, Brine's indifference from when we were children turned into the last thread of the family he had. If I'd tried explaining to him why I was leaving, it would have been like talking to a wall."

"Well, the guy had serious issues." Phoenix hummed, though his tone was still the same as before. "I can understand the logic behind your decision."

I nodded as I looked at Phoenix; his eyes were faintly glowing in the dim lighting of the room.

"I know I was trying to make an impossible decision." I said. "That's why I left Avery in charge. He was the closest to Luka out of any of us, being his partner and all, so I trusted him to make the actual decisions for the Group while Brine played 'leader'."

I looked at my hands, thinking of all the moves that had been made and how easily everything could have come crashing down if I'd made the wrong decision.

A pair of familiar hands, the palms rough with gun-worn callouses, gently pulled my face up to look me in the eye. His thumbs gently caressed my cheeks.

Phoenix didn't say a word, his eyes drifting over mine. His eyes were glowing embers of gold in the dim light of that room; they looked like those of a wolf, his pupils dilated. His dark hair was soft in soft waves now; it had been months since either of us had a proper haircut. He looked a little more grown up, especially with the stubble growing in.

I felt like I was seeing all of his features for the first time, and the details that made mental notes of themselves made my heartbeat faster.

I hardly thought that this was the time for such thoughts, especially with how hectic everything was about to get.

"Fuck it." I muttered.

Phoenix raised an eyebrow, but I didn't give him time to ask any more questions before I leaned in to press my lips against his. His body tensed, but to my relief, he relaxed and returned the kiss. He was so close that I could hear the growl in his throat. His heavy breathing told me he was fighting himself.

I'd been about to pull back, to reassure him that this was okay, but he pushed back, laying me flat on my back against the flat mattress. It was when he interlaced his fingers in mine that he pulled back, red blooming across his face as he let out excited huffs of breath.

"S-Sorry..." He said. "Wolf instincts... you know?"

He'd been about to move, but I stopped him, unthreading my fingers from his and putting a hand on his cheek. He let out a shutter as he looked at me, holding his breath as he waited for me to say something.

"You don't have to stop." I whispered, the words coming out in a breath.

I traced the bone structure of his cheeks and his jaw, and then my thumb traced his lips, his hot breath fanning against my palm. He gently took my hand and panted as he pressed fervent kisses on my palm and up my arm. I closed my eyes as he made the jump from my forearm to my shoulder and kissed along my neck. The spot around my pulse made my head dip back, and I could tell that Phoenix was enjoying my reaction.

He paused, his hot breath clinging to my neck, and then he dragged his tongue along my pulse. The action forced a moan from my throat, and his lips curved into a grin.

"P-Phoenix..." I breathed.

"I have to mark you." He murmured, burying his nose in the crook of my neck. "Please, Xy..."

When his eyes met mine, they were hazy, his pupils big enough to show me just what lay behind them.

Passion.

Desire.

Lust.

It seemed like he was begging for more than just to mark me. Heat pulsated from him like a heartbeat, and my heart raced to match the pace.

I realized then just how much I wanted this, and that realization set my veins ablaze with that same heat. I reached up, gently curling my fingers through his hair.

"Yes."

His fingers slipped under my shirt, softly molding my flesh as he dragged his canines over my neck. My heart sped with anticipation as he nibbled on the place just below my ear, causing another moan to escape my lips. His lips curved into another smile against my neck as he continued to nibble. As he did so, he ran his fingers further up my torso, sending pleasant shivers down my spine. My shirt rode up as his fingers went further, looping around my chest to fiddle with the clasp of my bra. He took my shirt and bra off slowly, peeling off each layer like slowly a blooming rose, and he pressed soft kisses against my collarbone. All I could do was watch as he showed attention to every part of my upper body. Heat bloomed in my cheeks as he went lower and lower. It was all I could do to not move as he neared the spot just above my thighs. Even at my slightest flinch, I could tell that Phoenix was reveling in my reaction.

"Y-You're being rather slow." I stuttered as I squirmed. "I-I thought you were going to mark me."

He looked at me with a soft yet teasing smile.

"Give me time, my belladonna." He said, running his hands under my thigh. "I'm already trying not to go feral."

The second comment made me blush; the thought of him succumbing to base carnal instincts being a rather... curious scenario... but it was something he said before that made me turn my eyes from him.

"Belladonna?" I muttered. "Like the toxic flower...?"

"A beautiful and deadly flower." He said, leaning up to turn my head to face him again. "And you're my belladonna."

"Yeah, a flower that's highly poisonous—"

"To those who handle it without proper care." He said, his eye piercing mine as he spoke. "When handled and cultivated properly, it's the most beautiful flower. Much like wolfsbane."

I raised an eyebrow at him as he continued to place kisses down my sternum to my belly once more.

"Then... does that make you my wolfsbane?" I hummed softly as light moans escaped my throat.

He looked up at me again and smiled softly.

"If you'll let me be yours."

I couldn't say anything, not with how muddled my brain was becoming because of his affection and attention. I watched Phoenix as he continued lower once more, stopping at the place just above my waistline.

I bit my lip as he stared at what he'd already exposed.

"You're staring." I said.

"It's hard not to." He said with a boyish smile.

I hummed softly and tangled my legs with his. I leaned up and flipped us over. He was a bit surprised, especially with how timid I'd been.

"I find it unfair that I'm the only one getting stripped here." I said, my white hair spilling over my shoulder as I leaned down to kiss him, only to stop as I danced my fingers down his sides and to the hem of his shirt.

This time, it was Phoenix's cheeks that were flushed with color, and I knew why. I could feel it pressing against my belly.

He was aroused, and probably had been since this encounter had started.

He was eager, and yet, he'd gone slow. He wanted this to mean something.

My heart was racing, not just with anticipation but also with desire; I wanted this to mean something, too.

I slipped my fingers under his shirt and slowly pulled it over his head.

When I saw his torso, I couldn't help but notice the scars, old and new. I ran my fingers over the discoloration of each mark, admiring the contours of each jagged line that met subtle curves of muscle. I didn't realize just how built he was.

"Now, you're the one who's staring." Phoenix said, a weak smirk playing on his lips as his hand massaged the backs of my thighs.

"It's hard not to." I repeated, leaning down to press gentle kisses against each of his scars.

Phoenix's fingers slowly moved from my clothed thighs to the bare skin of my waist. He flipped us again and pressed his lips against mine in a fervent kiss. It was a lot more heated than before, and my heart raced to keep up as my fingers tangled in his hair. His fingers tugged at the waistband of my jeans, whining softly into the kiss as if to ask permission.

'Even after such a display of passion, he still has the self control to be a gentleman.' I thought.

I pulled away and looked at him, his hot breath meeting mine as his eyes held a glimmer of pleading.

"Please, Xy—"

"You don't need to ask permission again." I said, gently cupping his cheek.

Those words were all he needed to quickly strip me of my jeans as he turned his head, breathing heavily into my palm. He was trying to keep his fangs from growing.

He was barely holding it together.

Soon, my legs were free of my jeans and wrapped around his waist as he buried himself with deep and steadily paced strokes. The pain had long since subsided, and jolts of pleasure rippled through my nerves like electricity. Phoenix was still restraining himself, which I was thankful for, but it appeared he was doing it for his own sake as much as mine. His breath was hot against my neck, his teeth gently latched onto the spot he'd found before. Each movement dared his teeth to sink deeper, darkening the mark he'd made.

Pleasure pooled in my belly, tightening into a coiled knot as his thrusts became quicker. I dug my nails into his back as I leaned my head back into the mattress. Breath was forced from my lungs in loud moans as he carved himself deeper into my core. His hand that had been on my thigh circled around my waist as he groaned, pushing himself deeper, and his grunts turned into deep growls that emanated from his throat.

With one final push, warmth flooded my belly and white sparks of light spotted in my vision as every muscle seized. My toes curled at the rippling ecstasy that tore through my veins.

Phoenix huffed softly, finally detaching his teeth from my neck. His breath warmed the mark he'd made, sending chills down my spine and prickling my sweat-slicked skin.

In the dim lighting of that room, we laid with each other, tangled together in a mess of musty sheets, not that we minded it. Phoenix stroked my back, tracing the mark of my wing, as I traced patterns around the scars he had. I could feel his heart pounding in his chest; he was still coming down from his high.

In all honesty, my head was still spinning, too; it had been my first time, and I'd run purely on instinct.

I'd never been focused on relationships or sex, given that I'd once been so focused on achieving Luka's goal.

My cheeks flushed with heat, remembering how the pain had quickly turned to pleasure, and how chasing that ecstasy was incredible.

"What are you thinking about, Xy?" He hummed softly as his calloused fingers moved to play with the still-dark ends of my hair.

"Nothing much," I hummed in return. "Never thought sex would feel like that. That was incredible."

"You say that like it was your first time." Phoenix said.

"It was." I said bluntly, causing his body to flinch underneath me; I looked at him. "Phoenix?"

"You're telling me *that* was your first time?!" He hissed, sounding almost mortified.

"Uh... yeah?" I said, raising an eyebrow at him. "Did you think I was having sex during my time as leader of the Group? Avery was, and still is, practically a father to me, and back then, no one in the Group really caught my attention, anyway."

Phoenix's face didn't regain any of its color; I didn't understand what he was so freaked out about.

"Phoenix—"

"Why didn't you tell me?" He asked. "I-I would have—"

"Phoenix." I said, straddling his body as I put my hand on his cheek. "Relax. I didn't tell you because I didn't think it mattered."

The wolf-shifter seemed to slowly relax as he gently took my hand in his, pressing his lips against my palm.

"And... you're okay?" He muttered. "I mean... I didn't hurt you?"

"I'm fine, Phoenix." I smiled softly. "I promise."

With those words, his body finally seemed to breathe with ease, and he laid his head back.

He looked... oddly relieved.

"Were you seriously that worried?" I asked.

"Y-yeah... sorry..." he said. "I'm... actually surprised that I didn't pick up on it..."

"Is that something that can normally be picked up by the Bond?"

"I... actually don't know." He said. "*Animae nexum* is all instinct. It's different with every person and every couple, so there are a lot of unknowns."

I hummed softly and leaned down, draping my arms across his chest and laying my chin on my knuckles.

"Will you tell me more about wolf-shifter culture?" I asked. "All the wolf-shifters in the Group, like Avery, don't belong to a pack. They were born in the city, away from the community. So... I want to learn."

He looked at me, and a tired smile spread across his lips. He gently caressed my cheek, running his thumb over my cheekbone with the most tender gesture.

"Anything for my Luna."

20

THE WOMAN IN THE RIDING CLOAK

Lexy

GODS, I WAS STARVING; Joshuah's order to starve me out was hell, especially with being pregnant. The baby moving in my belly wasn't helping me, either.

My terror was slowly getting to me in my isolation; I was terrified that one day... I would stop feeling the baby move.

The fear brought a sob to my throat, and I curled up as much as my belly would allow. Tears brimmed, blurring my vision as I prayed to the Gods' Tree that this confinement would end soon.

That I could be free.

That I could see Jaye.

That the baby would be born happy and healthy.

That I could raise this baby with Jaye away from the danger of Joshuah's tyranny.

I grasped tightly at those memories of me and Jaye under the Tree, the memory of what he looked like and how kind he was.

But... it all seemed like it was an unattainable dream now.

My fingers curled into the sheets of my bed as my tears slid down my nose, dripping from the bridge and soaking into my pillow.

'Jaye...' I gritted my teeth, a growl of hunger tearing through my stomach. 'Phoenix... Xyla... anyone, please... help us..."

I put my hand on my belly, relieved that the baby still responded to my touch.

"This will all be over soon, my darling." I whispered through the pain. "At least... I still have hope that it will..."

Click-click.

The sound of the lock turning distracted me enough from my pain, though only by a bit, and I turned to look at the door.

I dreaded at the thought of who could be on the other side.

Was it Joshuah to torment me again and try to break my spirit?

Was it his puppets here to humiliate me?

Every muscle seized into tight knots as the door slowly creaked open, and a robed figure slipped inside before quickly yet quietly closing it behind her.

Long white hair spilled down her shoulders from underneath her hood. The figure looked as though they'd simply walked out of an oil painting in a museum. The robe she wore was a light blue riding cloak, and my curiosity was piqued, though my anxiety was still on the rise.

I could feel her staring at me from underneath that hood.

"Who are you?" I asked, my throat raw from malnutrition.

The robed figure reached up with pale and delicate hands and lowered her hood to reveal a *very* familiar face.

At first, I thought it was Areena, but then I noticed the woman's eyes; they were cyan blue, and they reflected light almost like marbles.

"You... have Xyla's face... but you're not Xyla... or her sister..."

The woman smiled softly and glided forward, her footsteps silent against the floor. Instinctively, I shrank back a little, and she stopped.

"Don't be afraid, dove." She spoke with a voice that was soothing, sweet as a bell. "I am here to help."

"Why would you help me?" I asked, my guard still up. "You don't even know me."

Her smile was tender, bringing a serene air to the room. She walked over to me, her footsteps not even making a sound against the carpet, and she gently took my hands in hers. My anxiety melted away at her touch.

"I know what I need to know, dear Lexishira Crescent." She said in a soothing voice, her smile becoming somber. "And... I know that the foul young man who calls himself Alpha is the one behind such cruelty you've suffered."

Her eyes drifted to my belly, and I admittedly felt overexposed.

"Fret not, dear." She said, putting a soothing hand on my cheek. "The child in your belly will live, and you will be reunited with your dear *animae nexum*."

Her words made my legs tremble, and the hairs on the back of my neck stood on end.

"W-Who are you?" I asked, trying to keep my composure. "How... how could you know any of this?"

"Let us just say," she said as she tilted her head a little to the side, "I am a friend of those who have now returned, and I am here to aid this side in their fight."

Her words were cryptic, but they made my heart skip a beat with a rhythm of hope.

Her words meant that Phoenix, Xyla, and my brothers had returned to the Den.

21

INTERNAL CONFLICT

Areena

I WANDERED THE CORRIDORS of the Temple, the glistening white hallways I'd grown up in since Hollum saved me from the orphanage fire. Members of the Rising stopped and stepped to the side, bowing their heads as I walked past them, and I returned their reverence with a kind smile and a nod.

A scripted response.

Charm them with a smile and they feel blessed because their savior has given them the attention they so crave, the desire to be seen and made to feel special.

And I was forced to receive such praise when I wasn't really doing anything for them. These people didn't really receive anything but false hope from the Rising.

I wasn't blessing them; I was giving them a false sense of security.

And every one of those fools fell for it hook, line, and sinker.

'What a trifle.' I thought dully as I turned a corner to leave the light of dawn behind me and walked deeper into the commune. 'How much more of this is necessary?'

The act was getting old, and I hated putting on that kind smile for such simple-minded plebeians. Those idiots were searching for an all-encompassing faith when the world was scamming them for all their worth.

They thought that they'd found stability in the Rising, but even the faith they believed in so desperately was a scam.

A lie created by Hollum with me at its center.

'How pointless their belief is.' I thought. 'Belief in a lie that will come to nothing.'

I walked until I reached a certain door — the door to the main office — and opened it. The main office, while a facade, was a study filled with literature on the history of Arboriah City and the Morgenstern family tree.

Presumably, Xyla and I were descendants of Lucien Morgenstern, our blood enchanted by ancient magick from the old gods. I didn't know how it could be the case, considering the bloodline died with Cassius, but the legend was enough for Hollum to create some bullshit doctrine to feed the followers.

Thinking about all of it made me rub the mark on my shoulder; it had been irritating me a lot as of late.

"What's wrong, my little dove?"

I looked up at the desk, where my vanguard was sitting, turned to the side. He was reading some documents, not even bothering to look at me.

"Are you not supposed to be training at this time?" He asked with a sigh.

"I tire of this charade." I said, my words leaving my mouth before I could even think it through. "What is the point of anything that we're doing when all that matters is the task of killing Xyla? Why bring such idiocy as 'devotees' into this?"

Hollum let out a sigh and put the documents on the desk. His eyes narrowed a little as he turned his head towards me; he was analyzing my movements and body language.

"Those idiots' blind faith is what we need." He said. "They are but fodder for our enemies, a shield to distract the world from what is the true cause of this cult."

Despite his words, he looked to be just as fed up with the ruse as I was. I didn't understand why the devotees were necessary.

And... why did I feel it so wrong for us to be leading these poor desperates just for our camouflage?

"Something else is bothering you, Areena." He said, sitting back in his chair as he watched me. "What is it?"

My muscles grew tight in response to his question; I hated how he could read me so easily...

Read me like Xyla could...

The thought of what I had to do festered in my brain, and I lowered my gaze to the floor.

"Areena—"

"It's Xyla..." I muttered, my eyes building with the pressure of tears. "Will... Will she really be trying to kill me?"

"She will." He answered almost immediately, not even giving me time to breathe after I finished my sentence. "Come here."

I looked up at him as he motioned me closer with a single finger. I approached him in his chair, my feet moving on their own. He gently took me into his arms, letting me curl into his chest as he wove his fingers into my long hair.

"Your sister will kill you." He said, pulling me head to rest against his shoulder. "After all, it's revenge for what you did. *You* were the one who killed all those children and the orphanage staff when you started the fire."

My fingers twitched, curling into his robes as bile rose in my throat.

Memories of that night were seared into my brain, and they resurfaced at the mention of what I'd done.

Images of those burning corpses of children, their petrified faces of terror and melting flesh, the shattered glass from broken windows.

I remembered the sounds of that roaring inferno... and I remembered hearing Xyla call out for me.

"But... she—"

"Xyla is not your true twin, my darling little bird." Hollum said as he cupped my cheek, bringing my eyes up to meet his pinkish-gold eyes. "An unworthy man below her and her esteemed title took advantage of your mother. In her heartache and despair, she confided in me after she told me about the prophecy."

He brushed his thumb under my eyes, wiping away my tears that escaped.

This man knew my mother; he took me out of that place because Xyla and I had been stolen from her.

"Do I look like her?" I asked. "Like Mama?"

Hollum's lips spread into a gentle smile, but the twitching at his corners told me he was suppressing a grin.

"Very much so, my darling dove." He said. "Her same sterling white hair and her beautiful face."

He gently combed his fingers through my hair, and he brought my head back to his chest.

I didn't fight his comfort.

"You alone are that extraordinary woman's heir." He whispered. "And once you kill that false twin and fain both wings, you will be the one to forever change the world."

I tuned him out as he babbled his nonsense; I'd learned a long time ago to not interrupt him as he rambled on with his incessant monologue.

I'd heard my role explained many times before, and no matter how much I hated it, I couldn't fight it.

I was meant to kill my "false" twin and gain her wing.

I was meant to lead the world into a new era.

'Kill Xyla...'

'Lead the masses into a new era...'

I didn't want to kill my sister and become some mythical messiah for such dependent cowards.

But... I had to.

After all... I couldn't disobey my father.

22

AN UNCERTAIN PLAN

Phoenix

I stood with Xyla as she discussed the plan for the rescue of Lexy and the other imprisoned rebels with Avery and Brohm. Kaylen and Gerimy were standing with the unified rebels of the Black Wing Group survivors and loyal Pack members.

The plan was... interesting. I was surprised, given some details that she'd suggested.

"It's a risky plan, Xy." Avery hummed, stroking his stubbled chin a little. "There is a fair amount of merit behind it despite those risks, but..."

He trailed off, obviously having some of the same concerns I was.

"Are you sure about this?" Avery asked, crossing his arms as he looked at her.

"When did you become so used to using your ability?" Brohm asked, raising an eyebrow at her.

The subtle twitch of Xyla's fingers didn't escape me; I knew this plan was asking a lot of her, especially considering how she hated that part about herself for what had happened.

Though... I still wasn't sure why...

I'd never seen her use it, but she'd never explained why.

Xyla turned her to Brohm, and to my surprise, she simply smiled at him.

A *forced* smile.

"Not exactly used to it..." she answered. "But I can see the advantage it will give us in this situation."

"Xyla, are you absolutely sure about this?" Avery asked again.

"I can use it to distract Joshuah's forces long enough for you to free the prisoners."

I tried my best not to react to her statement. She wasn't answering the question, and she was making promises I don't think even she was sure she'd be able to keep.

"You shouldn't have to use it like this." Avery said. "Especially when you—"

"It's fine." Xyla said a little too quickly. She took a deep breath and then she squared her shoulders. "I'll be fine, Avery..."

It seemed like she was unsure of her own plan.

The older wolf-shifter let out a sigh and then nodded.

"Alright." He said. "But we only need it to get past the guards. The gear we took from the rebellion will come in handy."

Avery seemed to trust her decision, but there was still an air of uncertainty. Brohm continued the meeting.

"We'll have two teams." He said. "One to infiltrate and extract our captured brethren, and the second to get them to safety. If things go sideways, the second team will hold them back while the prisoners escape."

The air thickened with apprehension.

I knew what this was.

Everyone did.

It was a monumental risk, a potential sacrifice to save the bystanders who had been captured just for supporting me.

A twinge of guilt thrummed in my chest, causing my trigger finger to itch.

"Do we know when they'll be least expecting an attack?" Xyla asked as she gently took my hand; she'd noticed the tremor.

"20:00 hours, on the dot." Avery answered. "The guards change shifts every twelve hours."

"And things can be mis-communicated during the ensuing changes." Brohm added with a mischievous twitch at the corners of his mouth.

Xyla nodded and took a deep breath.

"We have our plan, then." She concluded and checked her watch. "We move out in two hours. It's best we prepare."

"Aye, ma'am!" Avery and Brohm saluted, and the entirety of their combined rebellion followed suit.

As the group dispersed, I stayed with Xyla as she leaned against the table, her head hanging slightly. I gently touched her shoulder, pressing a kiss against her temple.

"I know that look." I said, recognizing the furrow of her bow. "What's on your mind?"

She was silent for a moment or two as she looked over the intel that had been given about the Den and Joshuah's crumbling operation. Their ability to gather so much information impressed me greatly.

Xyla hummed and then leaned against me, closing her eyes with a sigh.

"Riding a bike..." She muttered. "Just like riding a fucking bike..."

She turned her head to look at me.

"I've found myself back in a leadership position..." She said.

"You wear the mantle well." I chuckled softly, trying to lighten the mood.

She didn't look amused, but I kept my smile. I put my hand on her cheeks.

"Xy, you're not alone in this." I whispered, touching my forehead to hers. "Let me help you with this burden."

She hummed softly, leaning against my hand. Her shoulders dropped, relaxing as she let herself be vulnerable. She caressed my hand, keeping it against her cheek.

This was her way of relaxing before the impending operation.

Enjoying the calm before the storm.

I gently pulled her into a hug, resting her head against my shoulder as I rubbed her back with tender patterns.

This was what she needed.

Comfort.

Affirmation.

Two things that she'd denied herself for years after Luka's death, even more so when she went off grid to look for her sister.

I tenderly nuzzled her hair, fighting the instinct in my bones to bury my nose in her scent.

"Phoenix..."

Xyla's voice was soft, sounding nearly unsure.

"What is it?" I asked, looking at her.

"How likely is it... that this battle with your brother will kill you?" She asked.

I should have expected her question, but even expecting it, it still made me take a mental step backward.

Unfortunately, I know Joshuah well; he liked to play dirty, and the revelation that he'd killed Sareena for the prospect of Alpha title made that abundantly clear. I didn't trust him to play fair in such an influential battle, either.

But I couldn't tell Xyla about my concerns, especially with her already so worried; in all honesty, she probably already knew my concerns.

I took a deep breath and gently pressed a kiss to her forehead.

"Fifty-fifty chance." I said, truthfully. "We'll be in our wolf forms, and the first to kill the other will win, or if an opponent shifts back into their human form during the fight, they'll be driven from the pack for their shame."

Xyla's fingers curled into his shirt.

"You'll win..." she whispered. "Promise me you will..."

My heart sank; I wouldn't hope to keep that promise, but if I said nothing, then she would know the depths of my doubts.

"I promise..." I muttered so that only she could hear the words, even though there was no one else in the room with us. "I promise."

She looked at me, and I let myself study her face.

Her shimmering magenta eyes.

Her smooth skin that seemed a bit more than now that her hair was back to white.

Her slightly parted lips.

My eyes lingered there longer than on any of her other features, weighing the probability of the battle to come.

"Are you going to kiss me, or are you just going to stare at me?" She asked.

A chuckle escaped my throat, and I let my hands drop to her hips. I pulled her into a soft yet passionate kiss. Her hands trailed up to my hair, and her fingers curled into my scalp as she matched my passion with her own.

When the demand for air made up art, I touched my forehead to hers. Her fingertips gently played with my hair, her breathing fanning my lips.

There were words I wanted to say, but I felt that saying them would be redundant.

Three simple words.

A fear in my gut told me that if I told her and she accepted, the tragedy would strike.

As it usually does in situations such as this.

23

UNFORESEEN CIRCUMSTANCES

Xyla

THE DIM LIGHT OF dusk settled over Arboriah City, casting the Den in tones of pinkish-orange and grayish-purple. The extraction team—which was composed of me, Phoenix, Kaylen, and Gerimy—were dressed in the gear Avery and Brohm had looted from the skirmish. It was a bit suffocating, and the gear felt a little tight, but I did my best not to complain.

Though... that didn't stop Gerimy from voicing his own protests.

"Gods, this is embarrassing." He groaned.

"Shut up, Gerimy." Kaylen hissed.

He luckily quieted down enough as we approached a group of unsuspecting guards, a group of three militants who were all apparently all too eager for the shift change, judging by the way they were pacing. They stopped when they noticed us.

Their gear wasn't too different from ours, though the headgear I was wearing hid my eyes, which Phoenix had insisted on.

"Oi, what's all this 'ere?" The leader spoke with broken grammar.

"Shift change." I said, making the leader look at me.

His brow furrowed.

"We just changed shifts." He said. "Oo arr ya blokes?"

I took a deep breath, focusing my vision on the leader.

"*We're here to relieve you.*" I repeated. "*Take a long rest.*"

The leader's eyes blinked a little, and his eyes glowed, flickering with a pinkish-gold hue.

"R-Right..." He slurred his words. "We do deserve a long break..."

"Sir?" One of the others stepped forward. "We just started our shift. We—"

"We all deserve rest, soldier." The leader turned, his hand on his gun, and he pointed it at his men. "*We will rest as this soldier had insisted.*"

Panic rippled through my nerves.

"Xy, what are they doing?!" Phoenix whispered.

My heart beat in my chest; I didn't know what was going on.

I hadn't even tried to push the thought that hard... why was this happening...?

"Sir, put the gun anyway!" The other three guards readied their rifles, but before they could even fire a shot at us or at the leader, he shot a single bullet through each of their heads.

Bang!

Fear froze the blood in my veins.

Bang!

Each shot reverberated through my skull.

Bang!

Each shot accompanied by the horrific sight of blood. The bodies all dropped to the ground.

"Dammit, Xyla!" Gerimy hissed. "What did you do?!"

The leader turned to us, a tired smile on his face, and he put his gun to his temple.

"I'm so tired..." He said, tilting his head towards the gun. "I think I'll go to sleep."

"W-Wait—!"

"I'm going to sleep now."

"Don't—!"

Bang!

I covered my mouth, that familiar taste of bile rising in my throat, and I looked away.

I'd been too confident... or rather, I'd been too careless. I fell to the ground with weakened knees.

"I-I just told him to rest..." I muttered.

"Xy, we can't stop now." Phoenix said, putting his hand on my shoulder. "We need to move."

"Like hell I'm going with this freak!" Gerimy hissed, his words hurting me deeply.

"Gerimy—"

"No, Kaylen!" He cut off his elder brother. "I'm not taking one more step with this—"

Phoenix's hand flinched, and he turned to grab the youngest brother by his vest, his teeth bared and his eyes fierce. Had he been in his wolf form, his lips would have been pulled back in such a fierce snarl.

"This *what*, Gerimy?" He growled through seething teeth. "Go on. Say it."

I stood and reached out to touch his shoulder.

"Phoenix—"

"Alpha, don't you see?!" Gerimy said, putting his hands on his leader's forearms. "She's a monster!"

Every nerve constricted in my limbs, and my blood pounded in my ears.

"Gerimy!" Kaylen hissed, grabbing his brother by the head. "Apologize, now!"

"Why should I?! You saw what she did!" Gerimy said, trying to reason. "She's no descendant of Arboriah Lux! She's a killer! Just like Eshrik Passor!"

My vision became blurry with hot tears, my head spinning with Gerimy's harsh words.

His words were more said out of fear than anything else; I knew that.

But it didn't stop the pain and shame I felt.

"What happened?"

Avery's voice cut through the panic in my head, and his familiar rough hand touched my shoulder. Brohm and the rest of the second team had come, and before Gerimy could say anything, Phoenix spoke up.

"Xyla's ability went out of control." He said. "The guards ended up getting shot by their own leader."

I closed my eyes and bowed my head, prying the helmet from my head. My white hair hid my ugly-crying face.

Avery's hand gently squeezed my shoulder.

"New plan." He said. "Gerimy will stay with Brohm and our team."

"What?! Why am I getting benched?!" He asked.

"You're the one causing a scene." Phoenix said calmly. "I agree with Avery's judgment."

I didn't say a word; I couldn't, not with those words digging themselves into my brain as I stared at the soldiers' corpses. Those bodies reminded me of *that* incident.

"Xyla, love." Avery said, that tone he used to like Luka's. "You can't get stuck in your head. You need to move."

"*Xyla.*" Luka's voice spoke in my mind, and my eyes popped open, my heart leaping to my throat. "*It was an accident, Xyla. You've not used my ability in so long... please, do not blame yourself.*"

Memories of blood on my fingers and the frantic adrenaline coursing through my veins resurfaced, and desperately I shook away the memories.

"Xyla, you have to go." Luka urged softly. *"You can't stay here."*

I gritted my teeth.

Luka and Avery were right. We needed to move. I let out a breath, trying to relax myself, and I stood up. I brushed my hair back, and I looked at Avery.

"Phoenix, Kaylen, and I will continue on." I said. "Since Gerimy doesn't feel comfortable with a 'monster' on his team, he'll stay with you."

"Xyla…" Phoenix said, gently taking my hand in his. "It was uncalled for—"

"No." I said. "Let him believe what he wants."

I looked at Gerimy and narrowed my eyes.

"He's just a kid." I said. "He doesn't know any better."

Gerimy's lips pulled back in a snarl, but before he could say anything, I turned away and started towards the Alpha House.

"Come on." I said. "We've wasted enough time already. We need to move before Joshuah tries anything."

Phoenix and Kaylen soon joined me, and while our element of surprise was gone, we moved with confidence and intent.

While it hadn't been planned, our setback provided a better distraction than the one we'd had in mind. Phoenix brought Kaylen and me into a room off the beaten path as Joshuah's forces ran frantically through the halls of the Alpha House.

"We're being attacked!" Someone called. "To arms! Protect the House!"

We waited for the armored footsteps to pass, and we planned our next step in hushed tones.

"Josh will have retrofitted the basement to fit all the prisoners." Phoenix said as he took off his helmet and gear. "Not to mention that it'll be more than likely overcrowded."

"Meaning it'll be heavily guarded." I said. "Or, at least it was until this newest development."

My chest tightened even as I tried to push what had happened out of my mind. A hand touched my shoulder, and I turned to see Kaylen with a kind smile on his face.

"Even if it didn't go as planned, your ability did provide an opening for us."

His words oddly touched me; they were so kind, and they put me a bit more at ease. I nodded a silent appreciation to him, and I looked at Phoenix.

"We need to get going." I said. "The distraction won't last long."

"No, but we can prolong it." He said, a smile playing on his lips.

I raised an eyebrow, and before I could ask what he meant, he took his radio and pressed the call button twice, the three times, and then two again.

'A code?' I wondered.

Not a moment later, a collective of howls echoed from the distance, and I snapped my head to the window.

"A countermeasure?" I asked. "But... why—?"

"I thought it couldn't hurt to have the extra support." Phoenix said. "So, Avery and I collaborated, and we pulled together some resources."

"A second wave attack?" I asked.

"No." Kaylen said. "It's a diversion, a game of cat-and-mouse."

I realized then that they'd planned this ever since I'd volunteered to use my ability; they did it because they knew of my reservations. Phoenix gently took my hand and smiled.

"Come on." He said. "Let's move."

It was fairly certain to tell when we'd found the door to the basement; there was a damned latch and padlock on the knob.

I growled at the sight.

"Well, this certainly got more complicated." I muttered. "We don't have time for this."

"I agree." Phoenix said. "It'll take too long to find the key, and even brute force is out of the question because the noise could arouse suspicion."

I looked at him.

"Could we jimmy the hinges and get the door off the frame?"

"No, the door opens inward." He sighed. "We don't have access to them."

I chewed the tip of my thumbnail, fighting not to grit my teeth. This was another complication that we definitely didn't need.

Click.

I blinked at the noise, and Phoenix and I both turned to Kaylen, who'd been kneeling by the door and had the picked lock hanging off his finger.

"Let's not waste time on alternative, less classy methods, yeah?" He said before dropping the lock and opening the door.

As he went down the stairs, I looked at Phoenix; he was just as shocked as I was.

"You didn't know he knew how to lock pick?" I asked.

"No, no, that skill is relatively new." He said, still dumbfounded.

"Phoenix! Xyla!" Kaylen called from the basement. "Get down here!"

There was an urgent tone in his voice, and it put my nerves on high alert. The two of us hurried into the musty dark of the basement.

The basement was like a scene from a war documentary; the prisoners were all huddled together, whimpering and shuffling in the dark. They were bound in ropes and dressed in solid clothes. The majority were severely malnourished, and some were too weak to react to Kaylen and Phoenix cutting their bonds.

"A-Alpha Phoenix...?" One of them rasped, which triggered the murmuring and weeping of other relieved prisoners.

But they seemed to stop when my presence was noticed.

"What is *she* doing here?"

"Yeah, she's the one they want."

"She's a monster."

I clenched my jaw at the insults, forcing the bile back down my throat.

"She is the Luna." Phoenix said, making my head snap towards him. "My *animae nexum*. I will not let her be insulted for her efforts."

I walked over to him and put my hand on his shoulder. I shook my head when he looked at me.

"Phoenix." Kaylen said after helping the prisoners get free. "Phoenix, my sister isn't here."

I blinked and looked at the eldest Crescent brother.

"Lexy isn't here?" I asked.

"Joshuah took Lexy to another room in the house." A prisoner spoke; it was a member of the Group.

I went to help him stand as he stumbled, and when he realized who I was, he froze.

"Xyla...?" He said. "You're Xyla."

"Yeah, but Avery is the leader of the Group, now." I said. "And... I am so sorry for Brine and his actions—"

"All that matters is that you're back." He said. "Luka's pupil is back."

The prisoners murmured amongst themselves again, and I looked at Phoenix.

"I'll get Lexy." I said.

"No, I will."

All heads turned to see—

"Gerimy?!" Kaylen hissed. "You're supposed to be with Avery!"

He huffed and looked at me.

"I... want to help..." He said. "I want to help my sister."

Phoenix looked at him and then sighed.

"If you want to help, then help me get these people to safety." He said before looking at Kaylen. "Keep them both safe."

The wolf-shifter's eyes widened and then looked at me, his green eyes glowing in the dim light. I looked at either of them.

'Both of us...' I wondered. 'Why does he look so shocked? He means me and Lex... didn't he?'

Something didn't seem right.

"Phoenix—"

The alpha wolf-shifter pulled me into a kiss, and I froze. I didn't know what he was planning, but something told me that kiss meant more than what he was saying. He pulled away and touched his forehead to mine.

"I'll see you at the rendezvous."

He ran his thumb over my cheek before pulling away and helping the prisoners out of the basement with Gerimy.

I was frozen, stuck in my own thoughts; what the hell had that all been about?

'Why... did it feel like—'

"Xyla."

I turned to look at Kaylen. He was at the foot of the stairs.

"We need to move." He said.

I forced the thoughts to the back of my mind, and I let out a breath.

"Yes." I nodded. "Let's find Lexy."

It was easy to search the rooms of the Alpha House thanks to the distraction Phoenix had planned with Avery and Brohm, but our search was coming up empty.

"She's your sister." I said, looking at Kaylen. "Can't you follow her scent?"

"I'm not a damned bloodhound." He said. "Even so, it's not that easy. There are so many scents here that it's difficult to pinpoint where hers is."

I could tell he was anxious, with his calm demeanor; she was his sister, and the more empty rooms we found, the harder it was to keep his morale up. I put my hand on his shoulder.

"We'll find her." I said, putting my hand on the knob of the next room. "We've not searched all the rooms, after all."

I turned the knob, only for it to turn against the lock. I looked at the door. This had been the only locked room we found.

"Kaylen... this door is locked..."

I got out of the way so that he could pick the lock; I was tempted to ask where he learned it, considering his skill. When the lock clicked, Kaylen stood and opened the door, and when we looked inside, my breath caught in my throat.

Standing in the room was Lexy, who was visibly pregnant, and beside her was a very familiar woman with long white hair that draped over a riding cloak and a pair of marble-like cyan blue eyes.

"Xyla..." the woman breathed, her eyes misting. "My dear, dear Xyla..."

I put a trembling hand over my mouth. The woman glided over to me, gently taking my hand away and putting her pale hands on my similarly toned cheeks.

"Look at you. You've let your hair grow out." She said. "You've grown so much, my darling."

Diamond-like tears trickled down the woman's cheeks, a sad smile on her lips.

The word that had been caught in my throat finally escaped, and it felt as though a weight had been lifted from my chest.

"M-Mother...?"

24

BONDS AND BROKEN BROTHERHOODS

Phoenix

I STOPPED JUST BEHIND the group of refugees at the edge of the forest. I felt a pain in my chest, and it made me look back at the chaos of the battle in the Den, the distraction we'd planned.

The pain was a sharp tug at my end of the Bond, a literal pull on my heartstrings. I looked at the Alpha House as the combined rebel forces still fought my brother's dismal ranks. The sounds of the battle were still echoing through the ghost town of the Den.

"Alpha?" Gerimy addressed me from a ways behind me. "Phoenix, we need to get these people to the compound."

"I know..." I muttered. "But... something is wrong..."

"Sir?"

"Xyla..." I said. "I... I can feel her..."

It felt as though her heart was breaking, and I could feel it. Something wet dripped from my cheeks.

Tears.

The tears I felt for her.

"Alpha, we must go." Gerimy urged.

"Gerimy," I turned to the youngest Crescent brother as I spoke, "get these people back to the Sanctuary."

"Phoenix, Xyla can handle herself!" Avery called out. "Trust in her!"

I didn't listen as I started running.

"W-Wait, Alpha—!"

"That's an order, Gerimy!" I called back. "Protect them!"

I didn't wait for anyone else's words; I immediately ran into the fray of chaos, pulling off the smothering disguise of black ops combat gear. I let my body contort itself, my bones morphing and white fur taking the place of smooth skin.

The transformation was much less painful now that I was used to it again, and I dipped down to run on four legs.

'Hold on, Xy.' I thought. 'I'm coming.'

I knew that running in my wolf form wasn't the best idea; I was the only white wolf, which made me *very* conspicuous.

But I was running on instinct, the instinct to protect my mate.

The instinct that gave me tunnel vision to the point I was thrown off balance by a shift in weight that sent me barrel-rolling off to the side.

A mass of dark fur, a mass that was a fraction of my weight, had tackled me.

'Gerimy?!'

My teeth bared as I growled at him; he'd disobeyed a direct order. The younger wolf-shifter bowed his head, but only slightly. The tilt of his ears and the tremble of his lips told me he was upset, and when he looked me in the eye, I had my answer for why he'd followed.

I'd made a rookie move; I'd gone running into battle without a plan and based only on a feeling.

I huffed, letting my lip rest over my teeth, and I bobbed my head. His ears swiveled, and he bobbed his head as well. I turned to look at the Alpha House; I needed to trust Xyla.

'And she has Kaylen with her.' I reasoned with myself. 'They'll be fine.'

I turned back and noticed a mass of tan fur hurtling towards us. I leapt and pushed Gerimy out of the way as the wolf tackled me.

'Fuck.'

The tackle had reminded me of the escape we'd made only a month before. There was that familiar pain I'd felt in my side and my shoulder. I stood and faced our assailant.

The tan wolf's honey-brown eyes glared at me, almost glimmering with a smug spark. I returned his glare with all the matched frustration I felt.

Joshuah.

'Fuck, we didn't have time for this.'

He snarled at me, taunting me through bared teeth. My frustration mounted, my lips pulled back in a snarl as my fur stood on end. There was a growl, but it didn't come from my throat.

We both turned our heads; it was coming from Gerimy.

He was standing tall, unafraid of Joshuah and his bravado. My brother turned to face him, as if daring him to make a move. My ears folded back as I growled at the young wolf-shifter.

'Don't be an idiot, Gerimy!' I thought, trying to convey it to him. 'Get out of here! Now!'

Ever so stubborn and hot-headed, Gerimy kept his glaring eyes on Joshuah. I saw how he reared back on his haunches; he was about to make the lunge at my brother.

The very definition of stupid.

I barked at Gerimy as he was about to lunge, but a singular, shattering sound that continued to ring in my ears as I saw the young wolf-shifter's body crumble to the ground drowned me out. Fur fell away as the body of a giant wolf shrank into the form of a young man, liquid red blood blooming from his forehead and pooling around his body.

Tears threatened to stream from my eyes, and I let out a howl of grief.

Joshuah's body language was smug as he turned back, his tail in the air like a fucking victory flag.

And the sight pissed me off.

He might not have been the one to pull the trigger, but he killed Gerimy.

I snarled in fury as the fur on my back stood on end; Tradition or not, I was going to snap his neck for what he did.

'Bastard!'

I lunged towards my brother, only for every muscle in me to spasm and constrict as I collapsed to the ground.

'Dammit... a fucking taser...'

My body slowly contorted back, the process even slower because of the current's effect on me. My white fur fell away, exposing my bare skin to the nighttime air.

"How sad..." Joshuah spoke, having turned back into a human as well. "You brought that kid to his death."

He walked over and nudged my body over, making me look at the sky as he smirked down at me.

"You're gonna die here, too, *brother*."

His expression was so smug that it made my skin crawl. I gritted my teeth as I forced words from my throat.

"Rite..." I groaned. "Rite... of Challenge..."

Joshuah raised an eyebrow at me before he broke into hysterical laughter.

"Oh ho! So, now you want the mantle!" He jeered. "Well, too bad, *Nicky*. You're going to die—"

"Tradition stipulates..." I said, turning slowly as I willed to stand; "that only the *first-born* of the Alpha can inherit the mantle, and it can only be transferred to another through the Rite of Challenge."

I stood tall in front of my brother, disregarding our lack of clothing in the dark; I was focused on his glowing eyes as fury brewed behind them. He glared at me with the utmost intensity.

"You are not the true Alpha, Joshuah." I growled. "I never *formally* passed the mantle onto you. You've just been a placeholder this whole time!"

"Enough!" He barked in return, snarling through gritted teeth. "You're just a coward! It took the death of a woman that wasn't even your *animae nexum* to break from your spirit! You don't have what it takes—!'"

"Sareena might not have been my mate, but she was my friend!" I said. "And you murdered her! You played on my guilt! Couldn't have been hard to do, considering you've done it since we were children, especially when our father spiraled out of control!"

Joshuah had been about to say something, but I jabbed a clawed finger at him, keeping my glare on him.

"If you want the mantle of Alpha, Joshuah, you'll have to kill me as Tradition demands! Single combat by Rite of Challenge!"

The surrounding soldiers froze in place, rigid with fear; even if Joshuah were to command them to shoot to kill, they couldn't take action because of Tradition. My brother ground his teeth together, his knuckles squeezing so tight that his tan skin turned pale.

He was backed into a corner; all wolf-shifters were bound by Tradition, and its will couldn't be fought or broken.

"*Fine.*" He growled, throwing his hand up to signal the guards to stand down. "I'll kill you in the Rite of Challenge."

He stood tall, but I knew it was only a farce.

He was trying to keep up appearances, trying to validate his false sense of authority. He wasn't the only one trying; I was fighting my anxiety.

This hadn't been the plan, and I was still worried about Xyla.

What had I felt from her?

Was she hurt?

Had she been taken prisoner?

I looked at Gerimy's corpse, his green eyes dilated and nearly red from the blood from his head.

What was I going to tell Kaylen and Lexy if I ever saw them again?

Joshuah and I were given clothes, and we were escorted back to the Alpha House; now that the Rite of Challenge had been *rather abruptly* declared, neither of us had authority.

The results of the Rite would determine the rightful Alpha.

And I couldn't lose.

I had to win, for the sake of the Pack and for the sake of Xyla.

I had to win and make sure she was safe.

'Xyla...' I prayed. 'Please... please be okay...'

25

BLOODLINES REVEALED

Xyla

ALL FIGHTING HAD STOPPED, but when the four of us heard the gunshot echoing in the distance, Kaylen suddenly became very anxious. We'd stopped to rest at the Gods Tree, and all I could do was stare at the woman who was my mother.

Ever since Mr. Graeves told me he and this woman were mine and Areena's biological parents, I'd had a hard time coming to terms with the decisions she'd made. Looking at her in that moment, there was so much I wanted to say, some of it not so pleasant, but I couldn't find it in me to berate her.

I didn't even know how I could accept either of them as parents when it was Luka and Avery who'd raised me.

"You have a lot on your mind." The woman's voice brought me out of my thoughts. "Speak freely, Xyla."

I fought the twitch in my eye; I hated how well she could read me. It reminded me of Luka... and of Phoenix.

"What are you doing here?" I asked. "Why show yourself after all this time?"

The woman had been sitting with Lexy, and she stood with a sigh; her posture was very regal, and considering her — or rather, *our* — bloodline, it shouldn't have surprised me.

"I am here because my daughters are destined to fight each other." She said, looking at me. "At least that part of my vision hasn't changed."

"What do you mean by that?" I asked, my brows furrowed in confusion at her words.

"Some things are not always written in stone." She explained. "As soon as you met Phoenix, I knew that something had changed, that he would be integral to your journey."

"Elita is the one who freed him from imprisonment in Cathedral." Lexy said as she rubbed her stomach.

"And you were here the last time when I was here at the Den." I said. "You were here, right under this Tree."

The woman nodded as she looked up, and I followed her gaze to the shimmering red leaves that gave off a soft light in the half moon.

"Yes, I came to give prayer." She said. "After all, I am the last *Aster-Blood*."

"Arboriah Lux was the last *Aster-Blood*." I said, my tone growing evermore defensive.

"Well, you're not entirely wrong." Elita said, sounding unnaturally calm.

Before I could say anything, she turned around and pulled her long hair aside to reveal a mark.

The mark of an eight-pointed star.

"Compelling evidence." Kaylen said.

"Agreed. That *is* a bit eerie, I'll admit." I said.

The woman turned back to us, a soft smile on her pale lips.

"The marks that you and your sister bear are similar." She explained. "But they are the marks of Heralds."

"Heralds?" I asked with a furrowed brow. I hadn't heard this part.

"Heralds for a new generation of *Aster-Bloods*." She said. "But the marks you have are incomplete. Only by gaining the second half of the pair will you be able to properly herald the new dawn."

"Will ya stop speaking in dan riddles?" I asked, pinching the bridge of my nose while trying to curb my frustration. "Give me a straight answer. What's so important about Areena and me? What *are* we?!"

The woman walked over to me, and I froze as she put her hands on my cheeks. Her thumbs softly traced my cheekbones in an affectionate gesture, which oddly calmed my irritation.

"You are the product of two bloodlines." She said. "The Morgenstern bloodline, my blood, and the descendant of Arboriah Lux, the last *Aster-Blood*... your father's bloodline. The culmination of Lucien and Adalaine, the siblings that were separated by tragedy. After years and years of the bloodlines being diverged, they had finally been reunited."

It felt as though a switch flipped in my brain at the revelation. I remembered what Graeves had said about his abilities as an Empath, and I recalled stories of Arboriah Lux and her abilities as an *Aster-Blood*. She'd also been an Empath, and a powerful one, at that.

"Mr. Graeves… is a direct descendant of Arboriah Lux…" I muttered, tears prickling at the edges of my eyes.

The woman nodded with a smile, though there was a somber curve to it.

"But… how is any of this possible?" Kaylen asked. "Mr. Graeves told us of your lineage, but I've been having a hard time trying to figure how it can be. Cassius Morgenstern's bride and child were murdered by—"

"Yes, they were, but he did remarry." She said, turning to look at him. "Cassius also had the ability to hypnotize and rewrite memories, though it manifested much later in his life after he married Avaline."

"Avaline?" I asked. "Wait, you mean the servant girl?"

I remembered how she'd been the one to give the warning to Arboriah Lux, how she'd also distracted the true culprit in order for her to free Esilas Solani and Elderik Passor.

"It was several years after the First Council had been established." Elita said. "In fact, it was Arboriah Lux who preceded over the wedding."

"Charming little fact aside," Kaylen said, "how is it you are still alive if you're the daughter of Cassius and Avaline? That was over three hundred years ago."

"I… am not entirely sure myself…" She said. "I am gifted—or cursed, depending on how you look at it—with eternal youth and longevity, and I can only assume that it's the magick in my Morgenstern blood being as potent as my father's. I was never able to ask my father or his family."

I loathed to admit it, but what she said made sense; it was common knowledge that the Morgenstern bloodline was powerful, not only in name but also in abilities.

"Magick passed through the direct descendants of Lucien Morgenstern gifts longevity." She continued to explain. "And it was discovered much later on that it reacts to astrological events."

"Wait, what?" I asked, the information throwing me for a loop. "What's that supposed to mean?"

"With my birth, in particular," she said, "I was born during a rare celestial event. A comet blazing across the night sky."

"The Cassius Comet." Kaylen said. "It first appeared in the sky during the year 1832."

"It's not the only example of this being the case." Elita nodded. "My father had been born during a lunar eclipse that coincided with the autumn equinox."

When she turned to me, I felt a chill run down my spine; I suddenly had a terrible feeling. There was a question that nagged at me, gnawing at my brain.

"And... when Areena and I were born?" I asked.

I'd never known when our birthday was; we'd only ever celebrated the anniversary of when we arrived at the orphanage.

"You and your sister were born on the full moon during the summer solstice." Elita spoke, though she did so with some hesitation. "You were born on the eve of my own birthday."

Kaylen took a step forward.

"Wait, what does that mean?" He asked. "I get the correlation, but what does that mean for Xyla and the prophecy of yours?"

That bad feeling was getting worse, simmering in the pit of my stomach. I thought I was going to be sick.

"There have been many jumps in the evolution of mankind since Lucien and Adalaine Morgenstern returned from their journey, bringing with them the magick of the Gods' Tree." Lexy spoke up. "The emergence of wolf-shifters, for example."

"Yes." Elita said with a nod. "Abilities have been found in certain combinations of genes and parentage."

"Like... being a Mesmer..." I said, the feeling in my stomach boiling into nausea.

I put my hand over my mouth as I felt bile rise in my throat. Kaylen's form sprung into action as I turned away from everyone.

"Xyla? Are you okay?"

His inquiry forced the vile fluid from my stomach, and I turned and leaned over, bracing myself against the Tree.

"Xyla..." Lexy said as she stood up, holding her belly.

"I'm fine." I said, wiping my mouth as I turned back to them. "It's fine. It's nothing. I... just think this subject is making me queasy."

Elita had gone silent, a shadow of guilt on her face; I recalled what she'd said about her vision, and I looked at her.

"Your vision..." I said, my throat raw from vomit. "What did you see exactly? What's changed? What is a Herald of Seraphim?"

Her fingers flinched, and she was biting the inside of her cheek; had she already seen the outcome?

Was one of us going to die...?

I opened my mouth to speak, only to be cut off by the rustling of bushes behind me. I turned on my heel, pulling my gun from the back of my waistband, and who emerged were Avery, Brohm, and a few others from his team.

"Avery?" I lowered the gun. "Geez, you scared—"

"It's you." He said.

His eyes weren't on me; they were on Elita. I turned and looked between her and Avery, my brow furrowed in confusion.

"Wait, how do you know her?" I asked, before looking at Elita. "How do you know *him*?"

Avery looked at me and bowed his head, rubbing the back of his neck.

"She's... the one who charged Luka and I with looking after you." He said. "She came to our house the night Luka found you and brought you home."

My heart leapt in my throat at his confession, and I looked at the woman in the pale riding cloak.

"You knew Luka...?"

Elita nodded, clasping her hands in front of her in such a regal posture. She took a deep breath before she spoke.

"Yes... I saw a vision of the life you would have being a part of Luka's family. I saw you happy. Protected."

There were so many questions I had at that moment, I didn't know where to start.

'Protected...?'

Was she the reason Luka knew about Seraphim?

"What exactly is going on here?" Kaylen asked. "Avery, where's Phoenix?"

The name brought me to my senses, and I turned to Avery; he had a look of guilt on his face.

"Avery...?"

He dropped to a knee, not looking any of us in the eye.

"The Rite of Challenge has been called." He said. "It was announced shortly after we got everyone to Sanctuary."

"What the hell?" I asked. "What is he thinking? This wasn't the plan—"

"There's something else..." Avery said. "Gerimy... he went with him to find you..."

"Gerimy did?" Lexy asked, still holding her belly. "Where is he? Where is Gerimy?"

Avery's body became tense, and he tucked his chin closer to his chest. I recalled the gunshot we'd heard... and the howl soon after...

I immediately understood what had happened, and Lexy seemed to understand as well, given Avery's silence. She crumbled back to the bench with a strangled sob. Kaylen's teeth gritted, and he screamed.

"Dammit!" He growled. "Dammit, Gerimy! Why couldn't you follow orders, just this once?!"

Elita walked over to them, and she sat with Lexy, who fell onto her shoulder as she grieved. I gritted my teeth, imagining the guilt the Phoenix was feeling, and I looked at Avery.

"Let's go back to Sanctuary." I said. "We need to regroup... and we need to drive for Gerimy."

Avery nodded.

"We were able to retrieve his body after they took Phoenix and Joshuah back to the Alpha House." He said. "The others are waiting for further orders."

I nodded, and I helped Elita with Lexy as we walked back to Sanctuary. I couldn't help but feel responsible for what happened, and that guilt stewed in me the entire walk back.

26

FUNERAL RITES FOR THE FALLEN

Xyla

IT WASN'T THE FIRST funeral I'd been to; I'd been to several over the years, from Luka to fallen comrades in the Group. I was certainly no stranger to the idea of death and the traditions and culture surrounding it.

It was, however, the first funeral I'd been to for a Pack member.

Tradition states, according to Avery, that a fallen member of the Pack would be put to rest by his surviving family members, set on a funeral pyre and cremated. The ashes would be collected into a vessel and buried in the family's crypt.

The Sanctuary was built underground, but it was equipped with a fire pit in the community hall, which could be used as a funeral pyre. The shaft leading upwards was well-ventilated. I would have worried about us being found out, but with the Rite of Challenge being called, a ceasefire was in effect.

No one would come looking for us.

Tradition forbade retaliatory action from either side.

I watched as the young wolf-shifter's body, adorned in hyacinths and white poppies, was carried to the pyre on a wooden stretcher by other members of the Pack. Kaylen and Lexy, both dressed in semi-formal clothes, led the procession.

I didn't feel comfortable watching the procession, not with the guilt weighing on me. I longed for the solace of Luka's voice.

"Xyla."

I turned my head to see Elita, her hood covering her face; considering the prisoners and how apprehensive they'd been of me, we'd all thought it best that she keep her face hidden. Oddly enough, no one seemed to think it strange.

I should have guessed that no one would notice, not with the grief for Gerimy's murder. The room held a thick air of grief and vengeance.

"Come." She whispered, turning to leave the community hall. "Let's take a walk."

I followed her, a sigh escaping my lips.

We walked through the twisting hallways of the Sanctuary at a leisurely pace; I hadn't realized how extensive the underground compound was. It reminded me of the Group's hideout.

I pushed the location from my thoughts.

The compound made me think of the Pit.

The Pit made me think of Phoenix.

And thinking about Phoenix reminded me of my worry and my guilt.

I stopped walking and looked at my hands; my fingers were trembling as the reality of the situation became clearer and clearer.

"Xyla?" Elita's voice called out to me from the spiraling thoughts in my head.

"I can't control it." I whispered. "I botched this entire operation... all because of this damned ability..."

I squeezed my eyes shut and dug my palms into my eye sockets, digging my fingers into my scalp.

"Gerimy called me a monster...." I said, my voice barely above a whisper. "He was right... because of me, everything went to shit, and he died."

"Xyla."

Elita's hands gently pulled mine away from my eyes, and she made me look at her. As my vision came back into focus, she gently caressed my cheeks. Her cyan marble eyes reflected an understanding and somber glow.

"You're not a monster, Xyla." She said. "The biggest mistake anyone could make about themselves is letting fear and insecurity conquer them. Over time, that fear will destroy them."

She gently brushed my hair aside, her words soothing as she spoke.

"You are strong. The descendant of Arboriah Lux and a direct descendant of Lucien Morgenstern." She said. "Let their strength flow through you."

Her words lifted a weight from my shoulders, and I felt pressure build up behind my eyes. I fought the trembling in my bottom lip. I could feel myself break down. Elita gently pulled me into a hug, running her fingers through my hair.

"It's okay to let yourself feel and be vulnerable, too, Xyla." She whispered, gently pressing my face to her shoulder.

At her words, the dam broke. I squeezed my eyes shut as the tears came forth, soaking into her cloak as she held me close. The dam had held back several years of tears; I'd never cried so much since Luka had died. Elita's touch was honestly so much like his, and I remember what Avery said about her being the one who asked him and Luka to look after me.

I could see where Luka got his caring touch; whatever she told him back then, he'd taken it to heart. I smiled softly and relaxed against her.

Was this what it was like to have a mom?

"And don't worry about your ability." She said. "It might be one that you didn't want, but it can be used to your greatest advantage when you need it."

I pulled away and looked at her. I'd been about to say something when she gently wiped the tears from my eyes. Her kind and caring smile returned, and there was a sense of pride about it.

"I watched my father train with his ability for many years before he and my mother passed." She said. "If you want, I can teach you how to control it."

My brow furrowed.

"How could I ever control it when I'm scared to death of it?" I asked. "Will it really be necessary?"

She was silent for a while, her present gleam seeming to fade a little. It almost looked as if she was dissociating. It went on for more than a few minutes.

"Uh, hello?" I muttered, waving my hand in front of her eyes; she didn't react. "Elita?"

A moment later, she blinked and then looked at me. Her eyes seemed to search mine.

"It will be necessary." She said definitively. "And the first step of learning control is conquering your fear of it."

Before I could say anything, she gently took my hands. There was an aura of hope that seemed to radiate from her.

"If you'll allow me, I could teach you some exercises my father learned when he was training himself to control it."

Had that pause before been a vision?

Why was she suddenly so filled with hope?

And... why did she also feel... sad?

27

AN UNFORESEEN CIRCUMSTANCE

Phoenix

THE RITE OF CHALLENGE was, by no means, a small part of Pack Tradition; it was a time for anyone who wanted to stake their claim to the mantle if they had the right connections. It was also a time where the will of the challenged leader was void.

Joshuah could not hold prisoners that belonged to the challenger, nor could he give orders to any wolf-shifter under his command.

It was the one time in any Alpha's life that he was as powerless as his challenger.

An equal, through and through.

However, if I knew anything about my younger brother, it was that he *hated* being seen as an equal to anyone, as weak as a newborn pup; the one upside to any of this was that he was bound by Tradition to not harm anyone affiliated with me.

That meant Xyla, especially.

Her scent had subtly lingered by the time Joshuah and I had been taken to separate rooms in the Alpha House, meaning that she, Kaylen, and Lexy had escaped before the Rite of Challenge was called.

I was thankful for that, but there had been a fourth scent I recognized, and I realized that had been the reason the Bond had been tight between us.

That fresh scent of midnight blossoms.

It was the only reason I could entertain, given Xyla's desire for answers. I bit the nail of my thumb.

The question was, what was that woman doing there?

What all did she know?

My thoughts swirled with curiosity and anxiety, and that anxiety was definitely not something I needed right now, not with a fight on the way.

'Both sides will be there for the fight.' I hummed in thought. 'And Xyla will *have* to be there. She's my mate, after all...'

My fingers curled into my palms, and then my eyes widened at a sudden realization.

'Whoever wins this fight gains the ranks of the other... and if Joshuah has been planning for this, and if the Rising is behind this... then—'

The door to my room opened, and I turned fast on my heel. There was a flash of white hair and a very familiar face.

My blood ran cold as I realized the set up.

That face didn't belong to Xyla, especially not with that hateful glint in those magenta-pink eyes.

"Fuck—"

28

The Evil that Drives the Enemy

Xyla

I HAD TOO MANY things on my mind as the people of the rebellion and I were escorted to our part of the arena. I looked at Elita as she and Kaylen helped Lexy walk. It was still a lot to take in; she was the daughter of Cassius Morgenstern, which made me his granddaughter and a direct descendant of Lucien Morgenstern.

The reason I had the ability as a Mesmer, a part of myself that I was still trying to come to terms with given how the rescue operation had gone. It had been nearly a week since the incident; Tradition stipulated that the Rite of Challenge be held on the full moon.

I guess it was a wolf thing.

I thought again about Elita's offer to help me train with my ability to learn to gain some semblance of control. I had told her I needed time to think about it. I wasn't sure that I was really ready to accept that part I hated so much.

But she insisted it was necessary for me to learn to accept it and learn how to control it without fearing it would push people too far.

I wasn't sure what she had seen during that vision, but it was enough for her to make a case and try to convince me.

She certainly was full of mysteries, this woman.

A lot of unanswered questions that she continuously danced around.

And then there was the question that had been raised about Areena and me being "heralds of the new generation."

What the hell did that mean?

I was still feeling nausea made me grip the railing, flexing my fingers around the metal pipes as I looked out over the arena. The place was a size of a small baseball field, the floor of which was covered in sand.

The two sides of "us versus them" weren't as evenly set apart as I thought, and it was obvious whose side was whose; across the arena from our group were the remnants of Joshuah's forces, and they were fewer than the members of our rebellion.

And there was a palpable tension in the air; it was nearly suffocating.

Everyone was already clamoring for the spectacle.

"No need to be nervous, Xyla." Avery said as he put his hand on my shoulder. "Phoenix will win this."

"It's not that I'm worried about that." I muttered, my brow furrowing. "I... can't shake this feeling that something isn't right..."

"What do you mean?" Kaylen asked as he looked at me.

"I'm not sure." I answered, my eyes glued to the empty arena floor. "All I know is that we can suspect foul play from Joshuah."

"Tradition demands that the fight be fair." Lexy said from a seal behind me where she was sitting with Elita. "But, you're right... I doubt Joshuah will be fair. The bastard has something planned."

The only question was... what on earth did he have planned?

Or, more precisely, what did *he* have planned?

"Welcome, everyone!" An announcer's voice boomed over the sound system, cutting through my thoughts. I looked up at the announcer's box; I could barely see him, but he certainly looked like a greasy little weasel.

'Where the hell did they find this guy?'

"Welcome to the Rite of Challenge! And oh, this is the Rite of our lives! Brother against brother! Sons of the late Nicholas Bryte!"

The crowd cheered on as gates on either side of the arena cranked open, and a familiar, transformed wolf leapt out of the opening.

I narrowed my eyes at Joshuah's tan-colored wolf pelt, how the bastard paraded around like a proud specimen. A white wolf calmly walked out of the gate below us, and I felt something twinge run up my spine.

The wolf was indeed Phoenix, but something didn't feel right about how he walked; it appeared he was... dazed...

Something was very wrong.

"Phoenix…?"

When his ears didn't even twitch, and my eyes widened. I gripped the railing so hard that my knuckles were turning white. I recognized those signs.

"That's—"

"Tradition demands that these brothers fight to the death!" The announcer sounded overly cheerful at the idea of them killing each other for some stupid title. "The one to overcome the other by the fang and claw will be the rightful Alpha!"

I felt my breath hitch in my throat; this whole thing was a trap.

'If Joshuah is in bed with the Rising on this,' I realized, 'that means that—'

"Let the fight… BEGIN!"

The brothers leapt at each other's throats, but I could tell that Phoenix wasn't really fighting; his stance was too loose, like he was a puppet on strings.

"What the hell is he doing?!" Kaylen asked from beside me. "Phoenix isn't some pansy! He's a hell of a fighter, so why is he throwing this fight?!"

"He's not throwing it." I said, practically antsy on the balls of my feet. "He's under a Mesmer's power."

"That would mean—"

"Areena is here." I declared, tearing away from the railing.

I'd been about to turn and leave to hunt my sister down, but a gentle hand clasped my arm. I snapped my head back to see Elita.

"Xyla, listen." She said, her cyan eyes reflecting urgency and desperation. "She's already long gone. She did what she was sent here to do, and then she left."

"But if I do nothing—"

"Phoenix will not die in this fight." Elita said confidently. "Of that, I am very sure."

I scanned her eyes, and I found mine narrowing at hers. Her eyes reflected a calmness that I knew wasn't forced; she was so sure about her statement that Phoenix wouldn't die in this rigged fight. I recalled her vision, and I felt a bitterness in my mouth.

"You knew…" I muttered. "You knew that this would happen."

"Xyla." Avery spoke up, but I kept my eyes on Elita.

"Tell me the truth." I demanded. "Did you know that this would happen?"

Elita's eyes twitched before returning to her calm demeanor, and that told me all I need to know.

"Tell me." I said.

"I… had an inkling…" She answered.

I jerked my arm from her hand and turned to face her completely.

"Don't play coy. You knew." I said. "You always withhold such information."

"Xyla—"

"No." I said, putting my hand. "You've hidden enough from me. I won't be ruled by your prophecy anymore. I write my own destiny, dammit!"

I turned on my heel and walked out of the arena.

"Xyla, wait!" Avery said. "What are you hoping to accomplish? Leaving now won't help Phoenix—"

"But staying here and doing nothing won't help, either." I stopped in place, turning to look at him.

"Tradition forbids anyone from messing with the fight." Lexy said as she tried to stand.

"Relax, Lex. I won't interfere." I said. "I don't even know how to stop mental suggestion like that..."

"Xyla..." Elita's voice was muddled with pity, and my frustration only grew.

"Gah, I need some fresh air." I said, turning and leaving the arena. "By the will of the Gods... maybe Phoenix will win this battle on his own."

I honestly didn't know what to say. Between Elita incessantly dancing around questions and my anxiety and powerlessness to help Phoenix... I needed to be alone before I lost my composure.

Even though the arena of the Den was an outdoor venue, it felt like I was suffocating. The tension in the fight's atmosphere and my own frustration certainly didn't help.

I was truly powerless.

Phoenix had succumbed to powerful mental suggestion, and I didn't know how to help him out of it. I regretted my decision to not let Elita teach me how to control my ability, and then I thought hard about it; would I have really been able to help him break it?

Even if I had the knowledge, the Pack's stupid Tradition forbade me from doing anything. I wasn't really someone to follow the rules, but I was at a loss for anything I could do; like I said before, I didn't know how to break such a hold over him.

I leaned against a fence, grasping the chain links to keep myself from pacing. I took deep breaths to calm myself, and slowly but surely, my anxiety ebbed away. I let out a sigh as I let my head hang between my shoulders.

"What the fuck are you doing, Xyla?" I muttered to myself. "Why did you even come out here?"

I relished in the silence and the solace around, a gentle breeze blowing my hair back a little. I felt like I could relax a little without all the intrusive thoughts. Even Luka was being silent.

"Well, this is certainly a surprise."

Every muscle in my body seized as I recognized the voice. I didn't even have to look to know who it was. I gripped the fence harder to keep my impulses in check as I stood and slowly turned my head.

Leaning against the fence a little ways away from me was a tall man with slicked back salt and pepper hair. He was dressed in a suit with a long coat and an ornate scarf with a certain crest embroidered on the ends.

A rising sun over water and two wings stretched upward.

It was the crest of the Rising.

I narrowed my eyes as I turned to face him.

"*Vanguard Hollum.*" I growled. "Or are you here as your alter ego?"

"I'm only here to watch, little dove." He said, taking a cigarette case from his inside coat pocket. "Here to see the turning of tides and the march of history being made. I'm not playing any part."

"Don't pretend that you don't take pleasure in watching what you do to people." I said, keeping my tone as even as I could. "You like being in control of the fates of other people. You have a god complex that matches that of Eshrik."

"Well, I'll certainly take that as a compliment, little dove." He chuckled. "But, truly, I'm only here to watch and see how this plays out. Seeing those brothers fight against each other... it's very similar to what will happen during next year's summer solstice."

I gritted my teeth at his proud peacocking. He was so confident that I wanted to smack him.

I honestly wanted to do more than just hit him. I wanted to kill him for what he did.

"What would you have to gain from any of this?" I asked. "You took away my sister and made her the face for your damned cult—"

"Correction, I *saved* your sister." He said, snapping his fingers and producing a small flame at the tip of his index finger. "All I've done is give that girl a family after you abandoned her."

"Bullshit!" I growled through my teeth. "I didn't abandon her, *half-witch*. I thought she had died in the fire that *you* set!"

Hollum hummed softly and looked to the sky, as if trying to find the memory of my accusation. He then chuckled softly.

"Ah, yes. The orphanage fire." He said with a nonchalant grin. "Perhaps my greatest work."

I fought the flinch in my nerves. I'd always had my theory that the fire was started by someone, that it wasn't an accident. But I never thought the man would be so blase as to actually confess to it.

"But why?" I asked, fighting off the memories of dead children and the fear and panic I felt. "What did you have to gain from any of it?"

The detestable man's lips spread into a menacing grin as he turned to me.

"Why, my daughter, of course." He said, his gold eyes flashing a bit of pink. "Well, that's what she believes, anyway."

My heartbeat pounded in my ears as nausea churned in the pit of my stomach.

"You manipulative bastard." I hissed through pursed lips.

"No, *you* are the bastard." He snapped. "You and that foolish girl, the bastard daughters of that naïve child of Morgenstern and that ex-black ops Cathedral agent, Oliver Graeves. To think that the tool of my revenge would be the descendants of those who caused *his* downfall... it's *fucking* priceless."

I gripped the links of the fence with one hand while the fingers of my other curled into my palm. My nails dug crescent-shaped cuts into the flesh of my hand, no doubt enough to break the skin, but I didn't focus on the pain.

I was focused on keeping my composure, even as I felt warm blood squeezing through my fingers. His words were nagging in my brain.

"'His?' Who the hell was he talking about?'

There was an inkling I had, and it made me even more sick to my stomach.

I must have had a countenance that gave away my waning composure, because Hollum seemed rather entertained.

"What a revolting display you have." He said. "You look like a rabid hellbeast."

He narrowed his eyes, his pinkish-gold eyes cold like permafrost.

"To think, that foolish woman thinks that *you* are superior to my Areena. How pathetic."

I pushed the nausea down in my stomach as I glared; I was debating my next move.

'I could end it all here.' I thought. 'Gouging those poisonous eyes out... tearing his throat to shreds... that's all it would take...'

"No, Xyla." Luka's voice nearly made me jump; he'd been silent for a long time. *"You don't know what he's planning."*

'Luka...?'

"Oh? Did I break the bastard?" He jeered snobbily. "Well, as much as I would love to do so, it's not my duty to kill you. That will be Areena's job, and then she'll bear the child of Seraphim... after I rewrite her memories, that is."

That one statement snapped me from my thoughts.

"Xy, you can't react." Luka's voice said. *"He's trying to get you to lose your composure, to lower your guard."*

I gritted my teeth, willing my anger back.

"What are you planning, Hollum?" I asked.

The man's lips twisted into a sickening smirk, the smoke from his cigarette blowing through his nostrils.

"You know, you and Areena both look so much like your mother." He said nonchalantly. "I sometimes wonder if one of you is really mine."

My eye twitched and more blood dripped through my fingers. Was this a ruse?

"Hell, I did get a chance with her. All it took was a trance to get her to submit."

I felt my anger on the rise, and the rage made my nausea boil in my stomach. Bile was rising in my throat. I slowly reached around to the gun I had in the back of my belt.

"You fucking bastard—"

"I wonder if *dear and sweet Areena* will moan like a whore as well."

"Shut up!"

I pulled my gun and fired off a shot with a *bang* before I could even aim.

"Oh-ho, I've made the mongrel's bitch so upset." Hollum sneered. "Oh, whatever shall I do?"

"You're gonna burn in hell before you even lay a grimy finger on my sister." I growled, gripping the gun as I took aim.

"Xyla!"

My head snapped to the side, and I saw Elita standing there; she was panting, like she'd come running in a panic.

Had she heard the shot? No, she would have had to have followed me from the arena.

"Xyla, you can't kill him." She said, her voice not its usual calm tone; oddly enough, it was laced with fear. "Not here."

"Why the fuck not?!" I shouted, my bloody hand trembling around the gun. "You have to know what he has planned! He's going to violate Areena!"

"Only if he succeeds." Elita said, trying to sound calm; in all honesty, she still sounded terrified. "He won't succeed."

"He definitely won't if I kill him now—"

"*Xyla!*"

It had been the first time that I'd heard Elita raise her voice, and it shocked me to where I staggered back a little. I still kept my gun trained on Hollum, despite all of it.

"If you kill him now, there's no telling what Areena will do." She said, returning her voice to a somewhat calm volume.

Elita's cyan marble eyes turned to Hollum, and they sharpened into a glare that I didn't think she was capable of.

"*Hollum Caldwell.*"

The leader of the Rising looked at her with a gleam in his eye and a bright smile on his lips.

"Ah, the lovely Elita!" The man spread his arms wide, as if he were expecting a joyful reunion. "How are you, darling woman?"

There was a foul taste in my mouth at his words; was this man seriously that delusional, or was this a weird gaslighting technique?

"I am ever repulsed by having to see your face." Elita spat; her disdain impressed and relieved me.

"Aw, don't be so cold, my dear." He said, his lips drawing into his usual callous smirk. "After all, that loyal dog of yours is dead. Though I won't be taking his sloppy seconds. Your daughter, Areena, is already my puppet, so she'll have to do."

My finger was already itching on the trigger, and his words only made my finger twitch all the more. Although, his words about her "loyal dog" didn't escape me.

Was he talking about Mr. Graeves?

Was he really dead, or was it a lie?

I looked at Elita; she stood proud and regal, but I could tell that her eyes glistened with sorrow.

"I will spend the rest of life as a widow." She said. "And when I meet my end, we will be reunited. You won't be able to take that away from me."

I was floored for many reasons, one being Elita's confidence in the face of the truth; did she not want revenge?

Then there was the information about the death of Mr. Graeves; how long had he been dead?

My heart sank at the thought that I wouldn't be able to see him again, and I could only imagine how Phoenix would take the news.

Hollum seemed to have grown bored, and he let his elated facade fade away with a groan and a roll of his eyes.

"You and your Morgenstern pride." He said as he clicked his tongue in annoyance. "What a pain."

He took a deep drag of his cigarette before exhaling a stream of wispy toxic vapor, before his lips drew back into a sickening grin.

"Well, I guess this does give me the opportunity to deprive the enemy of their advantage."

His eyes turned to me, and as they glowed, I felt my body become rigid.

'A trance? But.. I'm a Mesmer! How—"

I gritted my teeth as I glared at the man; this seemed to amuse him.

"Ah, your mental fortitude is greater than your sister's. Very interesting." He said, holding his hand out; with a move of his fingers, my limbs moved on their own. "But even with all that strength of mind, I can still puppeteer you around."

His enthusiasm was sickening, and unfortunately, he was right; I still maintained my free mind while he could control my limbs. I watched as the sight of my gun turned and pointed at Elita, and a realization of panic tightened in my chest.

"Now, be a good little bastard child and kill your mother." He said, his voice now commanding a tone as cold as ice.

My finger twitched, hovering over the trigger. I desperately tried to fight his influence and fighting the pain of that resistance.

"I-I won't..." I grunted through the pain, trying my best to ignore the sickening sensation of ripping muscles. "I won't kill her..."

I'd bit my lip so hard that blood trickled down my chin.

"Xyla, if you continue fighting him, you'll only hurt yourself." Luka spoke urgently.

'I won't kill my mother!'

"Pull the trigger!" Hollum demanded, his frustration mounted higher and higher. "Do it! Now!"

"I-I won't!"

"Stop resisting, you damn brat!"

"Xyla, please—"

"I won't do it!"

"Xyla."

Elita's voice silenced my two-way arguing, and I looked at her; her eyes were glistening with tears.

"It's okay, Xyla."

My eyes widened at her calm words, and my nausea was getting worse.

"W-What—?"

"Shoot me." She said. "You can't resist him for much longer. You'll damage your nerves if you continue."

Elita opened her arms as tears threatened to spill down her cheeks; it was as if she was welcoming the bullet. I understood, then, why she'd said what she'd said to Hollum.

She'd seen this moment as her death; she was ready for it.

But I wasn't.

"It's okay, Xyla." She said. "Shoot me."

"B-But I can't—"

"This is the only outcome in which things work out of you and everyone." She said. "It is a sacrifice that must be made."

Tears were building in my eyes just as hers were spilling over; I gritted my teeth to stop a sob from escaping my throat.

"B-But—"

"Shoot me! You have to shoot me!"

The intensity of her words startled me, and in my shock, I lost grip on my restraint, and my finger twitched over the trigger.

"I'm sorry."

It was an apology that was torn from my throat as a loud *bang* drowned out all the sounds.

All sound except for my heartbeat that was beating erratically in my ears as my chest heaved with subdued sobs.

The strain from Hollum's mental influence ebbed away, and I dropped my gun. My vision blurred with tears, but the sight before me forced a strangled cry from my throat; Elita crumbled to the ground with a red spot blooming on her chest.

Adrenaline coursed through my veins as I stumbled to run to her side. Blood bloomed its crimson flower across her dress around her stomach, and she looked up at me with the calmest eyes I'd seen in her situation. Her ever-growing colder hand slowly lifted to my cheek as I muttered apologies repeatedly, as if the words could turn back time.

"I'm sorry…" I cried as her cool fingers caressed my tear-stained cheek. "I'm so sorry—"

"Xy…" She spoke with a voice so loving, so forgiving. "It was the only future I saw… in which your baby lives…"

I furrowed my brow, and I shook my head.

"B-But… I'm not…"

"You are, love." She strained. "You're pregnant… a-and… you're—"

"M-Mom, stop… please…" I urged her to stop as held the gaping wound over her stomach. "I-I need to get you to a healer…"

A pained laugh escaped her lips, now decorated with spots of blood as she grasped my bloody fingers in hers. Her cyan-colored eyes began to fade.

"Y-You called me… 'Mom'…" she smiled weakly at me. "I-I'm sorry… for not… being there…"

Her words faded away, and Elita's body—no, my mother's body—became limp in my arms, the light having completely faded from her eyes as she stared up at me with a ghostly smile on her stained lips.

I stared at her corpse in my arms. Screams and sobs splintered the silence surrounding us, and I realized the reason that my throat was sore was that it was me.

A familiar pain and weight erupted from my shoulder.

My frustration and anguish, catalyzed by what I'd been forced to do, burst forth. I hugged my mother's body close as I squeezed my eyes, and a strange warmth enveloped me.

I didn't care about Hollum at that moment or the fact that he had made his escape.

I didn't care about the prophecy or the dangers it held.

All I cared about was the dead woman in my arms, the mother I'd always needed and that I was now mourning.

29

Battle Won But Much Lost

Phoenix

I'D BEEN TRICKED; as soon as I'd seen that white hair, I knew that I'd realized the danger too late.

She'd walked up to me, a sneer on her lips as if she was disgusted. She seemed so hateful towards me, and we'd never met before that moment.

My mind had still been fuzzy, and my consciousness was trapped as she commanded me to lose the Rite but to "make it look convincing."

'So, this is what it's like to experience the power of a Mesmer.'

My brain felt very violated, and I did not appreciate the mind-rape; I could see why Xyla didn't like the ability, especially with it being how I ended up being a prisoner in my own body, watching helplessly as my brother tear into my wolf's body.

There was the satisfaction, however, that Joshuah was getting frustrated; my body was healing faster than he was attacking.

It was the only thing keeping me alive.

'I have to win this fight.' I thought, trying to fight the Mesmer's influence which resulted in pressure in my brain. 'If I lose this fight, I lose Xyla!'

Fighting a Mesmer's influence was like trying to grab soap with oily fingers; every time I thought I'd had a grasp on my own will and movements, it slipped further away.

'I. Can. Not. Lose!' I willed myself to keep fighting for the group of my control. 'I refuse to give in!'

Suddenly, my senses perked at the sound of a loud pop.

And then, a little while later, there was another.

No, those weren't just pops; they were *gunshots*.

And a piercing scream followed them.

My chest thrummed with a familiar pain, and my lungs felt tight.

'Xyla! That's Xyla!'

A fire seemed to ignite around the Bond that connected us, and I felt invigorated.

That invigoration seemed to also lift the pressure and haze in my mind, and as I gained control again, I willed my teeth to bear themselves in a snarl.

Adrenaline burned in my veins as I clawed at my brother to get him off of me.

The crowd cheered as I stood, my wounds healing as my brother stared with wide eyes. His ears folded back as he tried to seem intimidating.

He growled at me, but his attempt at regaining dominance was feeble. I stood tall, my teeth bared in a snarl as I growled in a fury.

Joshuah had done more than sell himself to the cause of the Rising; he'd betrayed the Traditions, trusting in trickery as a means to an end.

And more disturbingly, he had taken lives; he'd killed Sareena, and he planned to sell Xyla to her death.

I let my rage guide me as I lunged at my coward of a brother.

I held my brother down, my large paw on his throat as I snarled at him.

Joshua's wolf form shrank, his bones contorting under my weight as he shifted back to his human form.

"W-Wait..." He coughed in pain from the pressure. "B-Brother, please—"

I growled and snarled at my brother, and he whimpered as he turned his head aside.

Joshuah was nothing but a coward, and shifting back to his human form didn't mean the battle was over. The Rite of Challenge was a fight to the death, and my *dear* brother was going to pay for all of his crimes.

The debt would be paid in blood.

Without another thought or even a regret, I tore into my brother's fragile human throat, his screams of pain muffled by the gurgling blood in his mouth.

My teeth found their mark, and with a swift jerk of my head, a sickening crunch splintered through the air. I pulled back, my teeth still bared in a snarl at the look of profound horror permanently etched into his face. His head was still connected to his torso, but the bones of his neck were crushed to powder, making it as floppy as a rag-doll's arm.

I stood as my body transferred back into my human form. Blood was smeared from my mouth to my neck.

I ignored the roaring applause and triumphant howls as I stared at my brother's mangled body.

'I never imagined that it would end this way.' I thought solemnly.

I would be lying if I said I didn't feel any reverse for killing Joshuah; for all the evil he'd done, he was still my brother.

I couldn't forgive his betrayal or deceit, but he was still family, my blood. But what mattered was that Joshuah's tyranny had ended, and Gerimy's murder was avenged.

Something tugged at the string in my chest, and I was reminded of what had broken the Mesmer's hold over me.

"Xyla..." I breathed.

I turned on my heel, my body contorting once more into my wolf form out of instinct, and I ran to find my mate.

"W-Wait, Phoenix!"

That voice belonged to Lexy, but I ignored it.

I needed to find Xyla.

I practically burst out of the arena, and my keen hearing picked up the shuttering cries of a familiar voice. I kept running, aware of the wolves behind me. There were two scents; I recognized one as Avery and the other was Kaylen.

We rounded a corner, and I skidded to a halt at the sight before me.

Rocking back and forth with a white-haired corpse in her arms and a familiar black-feathered wing draped against the ground was Xyla.

My heart jumped at the white-haired corpse in her arms; had she found her sister?

Had she been forced to kill her?

No, that wasn't it; something was off.

I cautiously walked over to my crying mate, and I made out words in her cries.

Heartbreaking words.

"I killed her..." She muttered through tears. "I killed her..."

I caught a glimpse of the dead woman's face, and my breath left my chest.

Her once-gleaming, marble-like eyes were now like dull, frosted glass, and there was a kind smile peacefully etched into her lips.

It was the woman from Cathedral who'd broken me out of containment.

And seeing her again, I realized why I recognized that face; that face was Xyla's... which meant that this was her mother.

I looked at my still-mourning mate, her cheeks stained with her tears, and I gingerly prodded my nose into her arm.

When she turned to look at me, my heart broke for her.

Her magenta-pink eyes that were usually aglow with a fierce fire were now flooded with tears, that fierce fire washed away, and her cheeks were flushed red. Hiccups escaped her throat as she tried to breathe.

"P-Phoenix..." she whimpered. "I-I killed her... I shot her... he made me shoot her..."

My ears folded back, and I tenderly like the tears from her cheeks. I sat beside her, minding her wing, and I tilted my tilted head back.

And I howled.

It was a Mourning Howl, and while it was usually reserved for members of the Pack, I thought it was necessary; Xyla was my mate, my family, and her family was mine, too.

Avery and Kaylen joined in the Howl, and other wolf-shifters joined in, too.

Her death wasn't the only death to mourn.

There were lives lost during the first uprising.

There were lives lost because of Joshuah's cruelty.

There were young souls like Gerimy.

And, even if I was the only one who thought so, there was Joshuah, the man he'd been before he'd been corrupted.

There were many lives lost, and it was time to properly mourn them.

The aftermath was chaotic; between organizing the relocation of resistance members to be integrated into the Den and ensuring that the prisoners of Joshuah's tyranny received proper care, there was a lot to manage. I relied a great deal on Avery, Brohm, and Kaylen.

Xyla and her grief had distracted me, especially because she'd silently insisted on mourning by herself. It wasn't just her mother that she was mourning, either; I learned from her that Mr. Graeves had passed away, too, not long after we'd left him to escape.

I watched from a distance as Xyla sat in front of the Gods' Tree; considering her mother was the last Morgenstern, she'd asked that Elita be buried there alongside the bones of Arboriah Lux. I wanted nothing more than to comfort her, but I couldn't find the words to do so.

"Xyla's life has been drowned in tragedy." A voice came from beside me, and I turned my head to see Avery, his sandy-blonde hair gently blowing in the wind. "The orphanage fire, the death of Luka, and now the death of her birth mother... I fear her sister will be the loss that pushes her over the edge of sanity."

I looked from him back to Xyla as her white hair wrapped around her shoulders as they jumped slightly.

She was crying again.

I hated to see such a heart-breaking sight.

"Phoenix." Avery put his hand on my shoulder. "You're Xyla's only pillar of strength now, her means of support."

I only nodded my head in acknowledgement, though I couldn't deny the chill I felt in his words.

"Aren't you a pillar of hers as well?" I asked. "You're still like family to her."

He gave me a sad smile and chuckled.

"In a way, you're right." He said. "But from Xyla's point of view, I'm only her adopted family. She found her mother and her father, but now they're both dead. She may feel like anyone she's close to will die just from association."

His eyes turned back to the crying daughter he'd adopted.

"She was like this for a short time after Luka's death... and the incident with the cop that had killed him happened..." He sighed. "She's gone through so much."

I looked back at Xyla, and I took slow steps towards her.

The task he'd given me broke his heart, I could tell; after all, he'd been a father to her, and now, he knew he couldn't be that kind of support anymore because of Xyla's mental state.

It was a task that I was more than willing to take on for her sake.

I loved Xyla; I loved her more than anything.

I knelt behind her as she cried, her tears a sign that she was trying to handle this all by herself, and I wrapped my arms around her, causing her to tense up.

"P-Phoenix..." She whispered, my name escaping her lips in a breath.

"Don't shut me out." I whispered, tears welling in my eyes. "Let me share this anguish with you."

I buried my face in her hair as tears fell. The reality of what I had to do in the arena reared its head in my mind, and I could only imagine the similarities between my situation and hers.

I had killed my brother, my only loving family.

Xyla had been made to kill her mother, a woman that she had only begun to know.

Her hands gently touched my arms, and I felt her relax in my hold as she let out a sigh.

"Am I destined to lose everyone I've grown to care about?" She spoke, her voice raw from her grief. "Luka... then my birth father, Mr. Graeves... and then my mother..."

She leaned her head against mine.

"Will I lose you one day as well?"

I nuzzled her neck as my tears fell onto her shoulder.

"Loss is a part of life, and life wouldn't be worth living if we didn't experience some sort of hardship to overcome." I said.

Her shoulder jumped, and a dry chuckle escaped her lips.

"How philosophical of you, Phoenix." She said, a faint smile clear in her voice.

"You know what I mean." I said. "If we are to die, when Seraphim comes... then I want to spend whatever time we have left with you... if you'll have me."

I gently took her hand, interlacing my fingers with hers. Xyla's shoulders jumped once, then twice, then thrice, and I feared she was going to break down into sobs. What escaped her chapped lips, however, were sobs more akin to laughter than actual cries.

She leaned against me.

"Idiot..." She said as she lifted her other hand to wipe her eyes. "Do you really have that much of a death wish?"

I chuckled softly and wiped her tears and my own.

"What can I say? I'm a hopeless romantic." I said. "And more importantly, I can't bear to see you suffering alone. It's only natural to support the one I love so much."

She hummed softly and then pulled away. She turned to face me, her melancholic eyes shining with a gleam of determination. It was a sign that the Xyla I knew so well was still in there.

"All we have is each other now."

She reached up and ran her fingers under my eyes, brushing away the remaining dampness from my tears.

"Why are you crying?" She asked.

A tired chuckle escaped my lips, and I touched my head to hers.

"Because... even after all of this loss, of loved ones being ripped away... I still feel so complete with you." I said. "I'll protect you with all that I have in me. I can't lose you, either."

Xyla's lips parted with a melodious chuckle, and she shook her head.

I blinked at her sudden change in mood, and I pulled back to look at her.

"What?" I asked. "What is it?"

She looked at me with her lip in between her teeth.

"Well, you don't just have me to protect anymore." She said. "Technically, it'll be *both* our responsibility."

I furrowed my brow at her words; since when did she speak so cryptically?

She then let out a sigh and gently took my hand... guiding it to her belly.

A jolt of electricity frayed my nerves, and I looked at her with wide eyes as heat bloomed across my face.

"Phoenix... I'm pregnant."

Epilogue

Xyla

PHOENIX COULDN'T KEEP HIS mouth shut after I'd told him the news; everyone in the Pack and the Group now knew that I was pregnant, and their attention was monumentally suffocating.

"You can't blame him for telling everyone the news." Luka's voice echoed, sounding amused. *"People need something joyous to look forward to with the loss and tragedy everyone had experienced as of late."*

'They have Lexy's baby to be excited about, too.' I thought in return, gently caressing my belly. 'I'm pretty sure I didn't need the mixed emotions of Avery to play tennis with each other.'

I looked at the small heap of dirt that lay underneath the Gods' Tree. It was a burial mound.

"I wish you were here to help me." I whispered to the wind.

The mound served as a tombstone for my mother, with white stones placed intricately around it as a sort of barrier, leaving a beautiful memorial that was perfect for the last of the Morgenstern bloodline.

'Luka... what did she tell you and Avery when she came to see you...?' I wondered.

He was silent again, which I guess wasn't surprising; he seemed to always fade in and out like an old radio signal.

I knelt to lay a few wildflowers at the foot of the mound.

"I wish you were here..." I repeated. "I have so many questions that I still need answers to... so many regrets I have..."

I ran my fingertips over the front stone, enjoying the peace of the moment as the wind blew my hairs behind me.

"You have no right to visit her grave."

My eyes widened at the familiar voice that seethed with hatred, and I snapped my head as I turned.

My breath left my lungs.

Standing at the foot of the path that led through the forest was my sister, and she didn't share in my shock.

Areena was glaring at me, her teeth gritting against each other.

"A-Areena—?"

"Don't say my name, you murdering bitch!" She shrieked, her tone dripping with murderous venom as her eyes reflected a glare of hurt and fury; I'd never heard her raise her voice, even when we were kids. "You killed her! You killed our mother!"

"Areena, it was an accident—"

"Fucking bullshit!" She screamed, hot tears running down her face. "Did you kill her because she left us?! Is that why you've done all these horribles things?!"

I fought to not let my confusion show, the confusion that bled into realization and culmination and fury towards the mastermind of this entire plot.

Just how much deception had *he* used to let her soak and stew in?

Areena's fury subsided into genuine heartache.

"Are you going to kill me, too?"

"No!" I screamed. "I wouldn't kill you! I've spent the better part of my life looking for you—"

"Yeah, to kill me!" Areena screamed in her returning rage. "He told me you were only looking for me to kill me! He saw you were murder our mother, that you said that I was next!"

"Hollum is lying to you!" I raised my voice, trying to convince her to the king of man she'd put her trust in. "He's been using you this whole time, manipulating you into being his tool—"

"Shut up!" She screamed. "Shut up! Shut up! Shut up! Stop lying to me!"

Areena's hurt turned to pure and utter hatred, and she pointed her finger at me as she glared menacingly.

"I'll kill you... I'll avenge *my* mother and kill you! You and that beast you've bedded!"

Her words were red-hot like fire pokers, and they dug savagely into my skin. She'd meant every word she said, fed by the lies of a disgusting man that planned on using her for his own twisted pleasures and schemes.

I no longer saw my sweet twin sister, whom I remembered from my childhood.

I saw Areena as the woman my sister had become: a woman molded by the lies of a man depraved of sense, her raw emotions laid bare.

I clenched my fists as I slowly stood to my feet, facing my sister.

"I won't let you sully your hands doing Hollum's work." I said, trying to save face as my heart broke and tears threatened to spill. "You won't kill me or anyone."

"And would you kill me in order to stop me?" She challenged.

My nails dug into my palms, crescent moon-shaped curves bleeding in soft flesh.

"I'll kill Hollum's presence in your heart and mind." I declared. "I'll kill the man who took my sister from me! The one who forced me to kill our mother!"

Areena and I stood our ground against each other, and the wedge that had been driven between us drove us further and further apart. Our emotions and ambitions were laid bare, but only one of us wasn't willing to follow through with murdering the other.

"Xyla!"

Phoenix's voice was cut through the silence, and Areena sucked through her teeth, almost like she'd been thwarted. She took slow steps back into the tree line.

"I'll kill you, *sister*." She vowed with venomous words as she glared. "I'll kill you for what you've done."

I stayed in place as I watched her disappear into the shadows of the forest, and as Phoenix and Avery broke through the treeline out of the corner of my eye, I fell to my knees, my hands trembling with my bleeding palms.

"Xyla! Xyla, what happened?" Phoenix spoke softly as he knelt in front of me, gently taking my hands in his. "Xy, your hands…"

I couldn't speak, any words that I wanted to speak being caught in my throat. Even with my tears finally following from my eyes, not even a sob escaped my lips.

"Xyla…" Phoenix's warmth enveloped me, his presence calming me as well as encouraging me to cry. "Oh, my Xyla…"

I closed my eyes as I surrendered to his embrace. I couldn't say anything; my mind was muddled by what had happened, past and present.

I'd lost my sister long before that conversation with her at the grave of our mother, or even before the confrontation with Hollum.

Areena had already been lost in the orphanage fire, and the woman I'd met was her ghost, a facade that masked the malicious nature that had replaced her sweet nature as a child.

She was a vessel of rage and retribution.

My sister was now my enemy.

My mother's prophecy came to mind, and I put my blood-smeared hands on my stomach.

She told me that this path was the only one she foresaw the survival of the life growing inside me.

Was the survival of this child dependent on something I swore I would never do?

'Will I really have to kill my sister... just so this child of mine will live?'

And I realized then as I remembered my mother's offer. She was sure that I'd need my ability as a Mesmer.

If Areena could use her ability as Hollum could with me, she would probably use it against me when it came time for us to fight. I would be at a disadvantage. I hated that feeling. I certainly would not lose to Areena and her conniving puppeteer.

I needed to learn to control it in order to survive.

I had to survive.

For Phoenix and for this baby.

***

End

(The story continues in Seraphim Requiem)

Also By

The *Aster-Blood* Chronicles
Arboriah Lux
Seraphim Awakening

About the Author

Born and raised in Alabama, Kathleen has always been a creative person. From an early age, she was drawing and making up stories to go along with her characters and creatures. When she was in high school, she wrote her first manuscript, but she never edited or planned on publishing that first story (don't worry; she does plan on overhauling the story and rewriting it.)

Years later, Kathleen started another novel project while working at an extrusion plant, and she started writing several others stories along with her first published novel, Arboriah Lux.

It has always been her dream to tell her stories and that they reach people, helping them to escape the pressures of the real world, even if it's only for a little while.

She still lives in her hometown in Alabama, where she reads, writes, manages her publishing company and her YouTube channel, and also visits the occasional anime convention.

YouTube: Kat the Crow-Winged Author

Facebook: Kathleen I. Lyons – The Author

Twitter: @kathleenlyons

TikTok: @kathleenlyons.author

Instagram: @kathleenilyons.writer